Sardanapalus A Tragedy

Lord Byron

BIBLIOBAZAAR

SARDANAPALUS,

A TRAGEDY.

BY LORD BYRON.

LONDON:

JOHN MURRAY, ALBEMARLE-STREET.

1823.

TO

THE ILLUSTRIOUS GOËTHE

A Stranger presumes to offer the homage of a literary vassal to his liege lord, the first of existing writers—who has created the literature of his own country, and illustrated that of Europe.—The unworthy production which the author ventures to inscribe to him is entitled SARDANAPALUS.

SARDANAPALUS,

A TRAGEDY.

.

In this tragedy it has been my intention to follow the account of Diodorus Siculus, reducing it, however, to such dramatic regularity as I best could, and trying to approach the unities. I therefore suppose the rebellion to explode and succeed in one day by a sudden conspiracy, instead of the long war of the history.

DRAMATIS PERSONÆ.

MEN.

SARDANAPALUS, *King of Nineveh and Assyria, &c.*
ARBACES, *the Mede who aspired to the Throne.*
BELESES, *a Chaldean and Soothsayer.*
SALEMENES, *the King's Brother-in-law.*
ALTADA, *an Assyrian Officer of the Palace.*
PANIA.
ZAMES.
SFERO.
BALEA.

WOMEN.

ZARINA, *the Queen.*
MYRRHA, *an Ionian female Slave, and the Favourite of*
    SARDANAPALUS.
Women composing the Harem of SARDANAPALUS, *Guards,*
    Attendants, Chaldean Priests, Medes, &c. &c.

Scene—a Hall in the Royal Palace of Nineveh.

SARDANAPALUS.

ACT I. SCENE I.

A Hall in the Palace.

Salemenes (solus). HE hath wrong'd his queen, but
      still he is her lord;
He hath wrong'd my sister, still he is my brother;
He hath wrong'd his people, still he is their sovereign,
And I must be his friend as well as subject:
He must not perish thus. I will not see
The blood of Nimrod and Semiramis
Sink in the earth, and thirteen hundred years
Of empire ending like a shepherd's tale;
He must be roused. In his effeminate heart
There is a careless courage which corruption
Has not all quench'd, and latent energies,

Repress'd by circumstance, but not destroy'd—
Steep'd, but not drown'd, in deep voluptuousness.
If born a peasant, he had been a man
To have reach'd an empire; to an empire born,
He will bequeath none; nothing but a name,
Which his sons will not prize in heritage:—
Yet, not all lost, even yet he may redeem
His sloth and shame, by only being that
Which he should be, as easily as the thing
He should not be and is. Were it less toil
To sway his nations than consume his life?
To head an army than to rule a harem?
He sweats in palling pleasures, dulls his soul,
And saps his goodly strength, in toils which yield
        not
Health like the chase, nor glory like the war—
He must be roused. Alas! there is no sound
        [*Sound of soft music heard from within.*
To rouse him short of thunder. Hark! the lute,
The lyre, the timbrel; the lascivious tinklings
Of lulling instruments, the softening voices
Of women, and of beings less than women,
Must chime in to the echo of his revel,
While the great king of all we know of earth

Lolls crown'd with roses, and his diadem
Lies negligently by to be caught up
By the first manly hand which dares to snatch it.
Lo, where they come! already I perceive
The reeking odours of the perfumed trains,
And see the bright gems of the glittering girls,
At once his chorus and his council, flash
Along the gallery, and amidst the damsels,
As femininely garb'd, and scarce less female,
The grandson of Semiramis, the man-queen.—
He comes! Shall I await him? yes, and front him,
And tell him what all good men tell each other,
Speaking of him and his. They come, the slaves,
Led by the monarch subject to his slaves.

SCENE II.

Enter SARDANAPALUS *effeminately dressed, his Head crowned with Flowers, and his Robe negligently flowing, attended by a Train of Women and young Slaves.*

  Sar. (*speaking to some of his attendants*). Let the
    pavilion over the Euphrates
Be garlanded, and lit, and furnish'd forth
For an especial banquet ; at the hour
Of midnight we will sup there: see nought wanting,
And bid the galley be prepared. There is
A cooling breeze which crisps the broad clear river :
We will embark anon. Fair nymphs, who deign
To share the soft hours of Sardanapalus,
We 'll meet again in that the sweetest hour,
When we shall gather like the stars above us,
And you will form a heaven as bright as theirs ;
Till then, let each be mistress of her time,
And thou, my own Ionian Myrrha (1), choose,
Wilt thou along with them or me ?
  Myr.   My lord——

Sar. My lord, my life! why answerest thou so
    coldly?

It is the curse of kings to be so answer'd.

Rule thy own hours, thou rulest mine—say, wouldst
    thou

Accompany our guests, or charm away

The moments from me?

Myr.   The king's choice is mine.

Sar. I pray thee say not so: my chiefest joy

Is to contribute to thine every wish.

I do not dare to breathe my own desire,

Lest it should clash with thine; for thou art still

Too prompt to sacrifice thy thoughts' for others.

Myr. I would remain: I have no happiness

Save in beholding thine; yet ——

Sar.   Yet! what YET?

Thy own sweet will shall be the only barrier

Which ever rises betwixt thee and me.

Myr. I think the present is the wonted hour

Of council; it were better I retire.

Sal. (*comes forward and says*) The Ionian slave
    says well; let her retire.

Sar. Who answers? How now, brother?

Sal.   The *queen's* brother,
And your most faithful vassal, royal lord.

   Sar. (*addressing his train*). As I have said, let all
        dispose their hours
Till midnight, when again we pray your presence.
                    [*The court retiring.*
(*To* Myrrha, *who is going*) Myrrha! I thought *thou*
        wouldst remain.

   Myr.   Great king,
Thou didst not say so.

   Sar.   But *thou* lookedst it;
I know each glance of those Ionic eyes,
Which said thou wouldst not leave me.

   Myr.   Sire! your brother——

   Sal. His *consort's* brother, minion of Ionia!
How darest *thou* name *me* and not blush?

   Sar.   Not blush!
Thou hast no more eyes than heart to make her
        crimson
Like to the dying day on Caucasus,
Where sunset tints the snow with rosy shadows,
And then reproach her with thine own cold blindness,
Which will not see it. What, in tears, my Myrrha?

Sal. Let them flow on; she weeps for more than
    one,
And is herself the cause of bitterer tears.

Sar. Cursed be he who caused those tears to flow!

Sal. Curse not thyself—millions do that already.

Sar. Thou dost forget thee: make me not re-
    member
I am a monarch.

Sal.   Would thou couldst!

Myr.   My sovereign.
I pray, and thou too, prince, permit my absence.

Sar. Since it must be so, and this churl has
    check'd
Thy gentle spirit, go; but recollect
That we must forthwith meet: I had rather lose
An empire than thy presence.

                [*Exit* MYRRHA.

Sal.   It may be,
Thou wilt lose both, and both for ever!

Sar.   Brother,
I can at least command myself, who listen
To language such as this; yet urge me not
Beyond my easy nature.

Sal.   'Tis beyond

That easy, far too easy, idle nature,
Which I would urge thee.   O that I could rouse
          thee!
Though 'twere against myself.

 Sar.   By the god Baal!
The man would make me tyrant.

 Sal.   So thou art.
Think'st thou there is no tyranny but that
Of blood and chains?   The despotism of vice—
The weakness and the wickedness of luxury—
The negligence—the apathy—the evils
Of sensual sloth—produce ten thousand tyrants,
Whose delegated cruelty surpasses
The worst acts of one energetic master,
However harsh and hard in his own bearing.
The false and fond examples of thy lusts
Corrupt no less than they oppress, and sap
In the same moment all thy pageant power
And those who should sustain it; so that whether
A foreign foe invade, or civil broil
Distract within, both will alike prove fatal:
The first thy subjects have no heart to conquer;
The last they rather would assist than vanquish.

Sar. Why what makes thee the mouth-piece of the
    people?

Sal. Forgiveness of the queen, my sister's wrongs;
A natural love unto my infant nephews;
Faith to the king, a faith he may need shortly,
In more than words; respect for Nimrod's line;
Also, another thing thou knowest not.

    Sar. What's that?

    Sal.   To thee an unknown word.

    Sar.   Yet speak it;
I love to learn.

    Sal.   Virtue.

    Sar.   Not know the word!
Never was word yet rung so in my ears—
Worse than the rabble's shout, or splitting trumpet;
I've heard thy sister talk of nothing else.

    Sal. To change the irksome theme, then, hear of
    vice.

    Sar. From whom?

    Sal.   Even from the winds, if thou couldst listen
Unto the echoes of the nation's voice.

    Sar. Come, I'm indulgent, as thou knowest, patient,
As thou hast often proved—speak out, what moves
    thee?

Sal. Thy peril.

Sar.   Say on.

Sal.   Thus, then : all the nations,
For they are many, whom thy father left
In heritage, are loud in wrath against thee.

Sar. 'Gainst *me!* What would the slaves?

Sal.   A king.

Sar.   And what
Am I then?

Sal.   In their eyes a nothing; but
In mine a man who might be something still.

Sar. The railing drunkards! why, what would
          they have?
Have they not peace and plenty?

Sal.   Of the first,
More than is glorious; of the last, far less
Than the king recks of.

Sar.   Whose then is the crime,
But the false satraps, who provide no better?

Sal. And somewhat in the monarch who ne'er
          looks
Beyond his palace walls, or if he stirs
Beyond them, 'tis but to some mountain palace,
Till summer heats wear down.   O glorious Baal!

Who built up this vast empire, and wert made
A god, or at the least shinest like a god
Through the long centuries of thy renown,
This, thy presumed descendant, ne'er beheld
As king the kingdoms thou didst leave as hero,
Won with thy blood, and toil, and time, and peril!
For what? to furnish imposts for a revel,
Or multiplied extortions for a minion.

   Sar. I understand thee—thou wouldst have me go
Forth as a conqueror. By all the stars
Which the Chaldeans read! the restless slaves
Deserve that I should curse them with their wishes,
And lead them forth to glory.

   Sal.   Wherefore not?
Semiramis—a woman only—led
These our Assyrians to the solar shores
Of Ganges.

   Sar.   'Tis most true. And *how* return'd?

   Sal. Why, like a *man*—a hero; baffled, but
Not vanquish'd. With but twenty guards, she made
Good her retreat to Bactria.

   Sar.   And how many
Left she behind in India to the vultures?

   Sal. Our annals say not.

Sar.   Then I will say for them—
That she had better woven within her palace
Some twenty garments, than with twenty guards
Have fled to Bactria, leaving to the ravens,
And wolves, and men—the fiercer of the three,
Her myriads of fond subjects.   Is *this* glory?
Then let me live in ignominy ever.

  Sal. All warlike spirits have not the same fate.
Semiramis, the glorious parent of
A hundred kings, although she fail'd in India,
Brought Persia, Media, Bactria, to the realm
Which she once sway'd—and thou *might'st* sway.

  Sar.   I *sway* them—
She but subdued them.

  Sal. .   It may be ere long
That they will need her sword more than your
       sceptre.

  Sar. There was a certain Bacchus, was there
       not?
I've heard my Greek girls speak of such—they say
He was a god, that is, a Grecian god,
An idol foreign to Assyria's worship,
Who conquer'd this same golden realm of Ind
Thou prat'st of, where Semiramis was vanquish'd.

 Sal. I have heard of such a man; and thou per-
   ceiv'st
That he is deem'd a god for what he did.
 Sar. And in his godship I will honour him—
Not much as man. What, ho! my cupbearer!
 Sal. What means the king?
 Sar.   To worship your new god
And ancient conqueror. Some wine, I say.

    Enter Cupbearer.

 Sar. (*addressing the Cupbearer*). Bring me the
   golden goblet thick with gems,
Which bears the name of Nimrod's chalice. Hence,
Fill full, and bear it quickly. [*Exit Cupbearer.*
 Sal.   Is this moment
A fitting one for the resumption of
Thy yet unslept-off revels?

  Re-enter Cupbearer, with wine.

 Sar. (*taking the cup from him*). Noble kinsman,
If these barbarian Greeks of the far shores

          c

And skirts of these our realms lie not, this Bacchus
Conquer'd the whole of India, did he not?

   Sal. He did, and thence was deem'd a deity.

   Sar. Not so:—of all his conquests a few columns,
Which may be his, and might be mine, if I
Thought them worth purchase and conveyance, are
The landmarks of the seas of gore he shed,
The realms he wasted, and the hearts he broke.
But here, here in this goblet is his title
To immortality—the immortal grape
From which he first express'd the soul, and gave
To gladden that of man, as some atonement
For the victorious mischiefs he had done.
Had it not been for this, he would have been
A mortal still in name as in his grave;
And, like my ancestor Semiramis,
A sort of semi-glorious human monster.
Here's that which deified him—let it now
Humanise thee; my surly, chiding brother,
Pledge me to the Greek god!

   Sal.   For all thy realms
I would not so blaspheme our country's creed.

   Sar. That is to say, thou thinkest him a hero,

That he shed blood by oceans; and no god,
Because he turn'd a fruit to an enchantment,
Which cheers the sad, revives the old, inspires
The young, makes Weariness forget his toil,
And Fear her danger; opens a new world
When this, the present, palls.   Well, then *I* pledge
          thee
And *him* as a true man, who did his utmost
In good or evil to surprise mankind.   [*Drinks.*
      Sal. Wilt thou resume a revel at this hour?
      Sar. And if I did, 'twere better than a trophy,
Being bought without a tear.   But that is not
My present purpose: since thou wilt not pledge me,
Continue what thou pleasest.
(*To the Cupbearer*).   Boy, retire.
                          [*Exit Cupbearer.*
      Sal. I would but have recall'd thee from thy
          dream:
Better by me awaken'd than rebellion.
      Sar. Who should rebel? or why? what cause?
          pretext?
I am the lawful king, descended from
A race of kings who knew no predecessors.
What have I done to thee, or to the people,

                                        c 2

That thou shouldst rail, or they rise up against
   me?

 Sal. Of what thou hast done to me, I speak not.

 Sar.   But

Thou think'st that I have wrong'd the queen : is 't
   not so?

 Sal. Think! Thou hast wrong'd her!

 Sar.   Patience, prince, and hear me.

She has all power and splendour of her station,

Respect, the tutelage of Assyria's heirs,

The homage and the appanage of sovereignty.

I married her as monarchs wed—for state,

And loved her as most husbands love their wives.

If she or thou supposedst I could link me

Like a Chaldean peasant to his mate,

Ye knew nor me, nor monarchs, nor mankind.

  Sal. I pray thee, change the theme ; my blood dis-
    dains

Complaint, and Salemenes' sister seeks not

Reluctant love even from Assyria's lord !

Nor would she deign to accept divided passion

With foreign strumpets and Ionian slaves.

The queen is silent.

 Sar.   And why not her brother?

Sal. I only echo thee the voice of empires,
Which he who long neglects not long will govern.
   Sar. The ungrateful and ungracious slaves! they
      murmur
Because I have not shed their blood, nor led them
To dry into the desert's dust by myriads,
Or whiten with their bones the banks of Ganges;
Nor decimated them with savage laws,
Nor sweated them to build up pyramids,
Or Babylonian walls.
   Sal.   Yet these are trophies
More worthy of a people and their prince
Than songs, and lutes, and feasts, and concubines,
And lavish'd treasures, and contemned virtues.
   Sar. Or for my trophies I have founded cities:
There's Tarsus and Anchialus, both built
In one day—what could that blood-loving beldame,
My martial grandam, chaste Semiramis,
Do more, except destroy them?
   Sal.   'Tis most true;
I own thy merit in those founded cities,
Built for a whim, recorded with a verse
Which shames both them and thee to coming ages.

   Sar. Shame me! By Baal, the cities, though well
      built,
Are not more goodly than the verse! Say what
Thou wilt 'gainst me, my mode of life or rule,
But nothing 'gainst the truth of that brief record.
Why, those few lines contain the history
Of all things human; hear—" Sardanapalus,
" The king, and son of Anacyndaraxes
" In one day built Anchialus and Tarsus.
" Eat, drink, and love; the rest's not worth a
      fillip." (2)
   Sal. A worthy moral, and a wise inscription,
For a king to put up before his subjects!
   Sar. Oh, thou wouldst have me doubtless set up
      edicts—
" Obey the king—contribute to his treasure—
" Recruit his phalanx—spill your blood at bidding—
" Fall down and worship, or get up and toil."
Or thus—" Sardanapalus on this spot
" Slew fifty thousand of his enemies.
" These are their sepulchres, and this his trophy."
I leave such things to conquerors; enough
For me, if I can make my subjects feel
The weight of human misery less, and glide

Ungroaning to the tomb; I take no licence
Which I deny to them.   We all are men.

   Sal. Thy sires have been revered as gods—

   Sar.   .   In dust
And death, where they are neither gods nor men.
Talk not of such to me! the worms are gods;
At least they banqueted upon your gods,
And died for lack of farther nutriment.
Those gods were merely men; look to their issue—
I feel a thousand mortal things about me,
But nothing godlike, unless it may be
The thing which you condemn, a disposition
To love and to be merciful, to pardon
The follies of my species, and (that's human)
To be indulgent to my own.

   Sal.   Alas!
The doom of Nineveh is seal'd.—Woe—woe
To the unrivall'd city!

   Sar.   What dost dread?

   Sal. Thou art guarded by thy foes: in a few hours
The tempest may break out which overwhelms thee,
And thine and mine; and in another day
What *is* shall be the past of Belus' race.

   Sar. What must we dread?

   Sal.   Ambitious treachery,

Which has environ'd thee with snares; but yet
There is resource : empower me with thy signet
To quell the machinations, and I lay
The heads of thy chief foes before thy feet.

   Sar. The heads—how many?

   Sal.   Must I stay to number
When even thine own 's in peril? Let me go;
Give me thy signet—trust me with the rest.

   Sar. I will trust no man with unlimited lives.
When we take those from others, we nor know
What we have taken, nor the thing we give.

   Sal. Wouldst thou not take their lives who seek
       for thine?

   Sar. That 's a hard question.—But, I answer Yes.
Cannot the thing be done without? Who are they
Whom thou suspectest?—Let them be arrested.

   Sal. I would thou wouldst not ask me; the next
       moment
Will send my answer through thy babbling troop
Of paramours, and thence fly o'er the palace,
Even to the city, and so baffle all.—
Trust me.

   Sar.   Thou knowest I have done so ever;
Take thou the signet.   [*Gives the signet.*

   Sal.   I have one more request.—

Sar. Name it.

Sal. That thou this night forbear the banquet
In the pavilion over the Euphrates.

Sar. Forbear the banquet! Not for all the plotters
That ever shook a kingdom! Let them come,
And do their worst: I shall not blench for them;
Nor rise the sooner; nor forbear the goblet;
Nor crown me with a single rose the less;
Nor lose one joyous hour.—I fear them not.

Sal. But thou wouldst arm thee, wouldst thou
        not, if needful?

Sar. Perhaps. I have the goodliest armour, and
A sword of such a temper; and a bow
And javelin, which might furnish Nimrod forth:
A little heavy, but yet not unwieldy.
And now I think on 't, 'tis long since I 've used them,
Even in the chase. Hast ever seen them, brother?

Sal. Is this a time for such fantastic trifling?—
If need be, wilt thou wear them?

Sar.   Will I not? —
Oh! if it must be so, and these rash slaves
Will not be ruled with less, I 'll use the sword
Till they shall wish it turn'd into a distaff.

Sal. They say, thy sceptre's turn'd to that already.

Sar. That's false! but let them say so: the old
         Greeks,
Of whom our captives often sing, related
The same of their chief hero, Hercules,
Because he loved a Lydian queen: thou seest
The populace of all the nations seize
Each calumny they can to sink their sovereigns.

    Sal. They did not speak thus of thy fathers.

    Sar.   No;
They dared not. They were kept to toil and combat,
And never changed their chains but for their armour:
Now they have peace and pastime, and the licence
To revel and to rail; it irks me not.
I would not give the smile of one fair girl
For all the popular breath that e'er divided
A name from nothing. What are the rank tongues
Of this vile herd, grown insolent with feeding,
That I should prize their noisy praise, or dread
Their noisome clamour?

    Sal.   You have said they are men;
As such their hearts are something.

    Sar.   So my dogs' are;
And better, as more faithful:—but, proceed;
Thou hast my signet:—since they are tumultuous,

Let them be temper'd, yet not roughly, till
Necessity enforce it. I hate all pain,
Given or received; we have enough within us,
The meanest vassal as the loftiest monarch,
Not to add to each other's natural burthen
Of mortal misery, but rather lessen,
By mild reciprocal alleviation,
The fatal penalties imposed on life;
But this they know not, or they will not know.
I have, by Baal! done all I could to soothe them:
I made no wars, I added no new imposts,
I interfered not with their civic lives,
I let them pass their days as best might suit them,
Passing my own as suited me.

   Sal.   Thou stopp'st
Short of the duties of a king; and therefore
They say thou art unfit to be a monarch.

  Sar. 'They lie.—Unhappily, I am unfit
To be aught save a monarch; else for me,
The meanest Mede might be the king instead.

   Sal. There is one Mede, at least, who seeks to be so.

   Sar. What mean'st thou?—'tis thy secret; thou
        desirest
Few questions, and I'm not of curious nature.

Take the fit steps; and, since necessity
Requires, I sanction and support thee. Ne'er
Was man who more desired to rule in peace
The peaceful only; if they rouse me, better
They had conjured up stern Nimrod from his ashes,
" The mighty hunter." I will turn these realms
To one wide desert chase of brutes, who *were*,
But *would* no more, by their own choice, be human.
What they have found me, they belie; *that which*
They yet may find me—shall defy their wish
To speak it worse; and let them thank themselves.

  Sal. Then thou at last canst feel?

  Sar.   Feel! who feels not
Ingratitude?

  Sal.   I will not pause to answer
With words, but deeds. Keep thou awake that
        energy
Which sleeps at times, but is not dead within thee,
And thou may'st yet be glorious in thy reign,
As powerful in thy realm. Farewell!
                        [*Exit* SALEMENES.

  Sar. (*solus*).   Farewell!
He 's gone; and on his finger bears my signet,
Which is to him a sceptre. He is stern

As I am heedless; and the slaves deserve
To feel a master. What may be the danger,
I know not:—he hath found it, let him quell it.
Must I consume my life—this little life—
In guarding against all may make it less?
It is not worth so much! It were to die
Before my hour, to live in dread of death,
Tracing revolt: suspecting all about me,
Because they are near; and all who are remote,
Because they are far. But if it should be so—
If they should sweep me off from earth and empire,
Why, what is earth or empire of the earth?
I have loved, and lived, and multiplied my image;
To die is no less natural than those—
Acts of this clay! 'Tis true I have not shed
Blood, as I might have done, in oceans, till
My name became the synonyme of death—
A terror and a trophy. But for this
I feel no penitence; my life is love:
If I must shed blood, it shall be by force.
Till now, no drop from an Assyrian vein
Hath flow'd for me, nor hath the smallest coin
Of Nineveh's vast treasures e'er been lavish'd
On objects which could cost her sons a tear:

If then they hate me, 'tis because I hate not:
If they rebel, it is because I oppress not.
Oh, men! ye must be ruled with scythes, not sceptres,
And mow'd down like the grass, else all we reap
Is rank abundance, and a rotten harvest
Of discontents infecting the fair soil,
Making a desert of fertility.—
I 'll think no more.——Within there, ho!

Enter an ATTENDANT.

    Sar.   Slave, tell
The Ionian Myrrha we would crave her presence.
    Attend. King, she is here.

MYRRHA *enters.*

    Sar. (apart to Attendant).   Away!
(*Addressing* MYRRHA).   Beautiful being!
Thou dost almost anticipate my heart;
It throbb'd for thee, and here thou comest: let me
Deem that some unknown influence, some sweet
          oracle,
Communicates between us, though unseen,
In absence, and attracts us to each other.

Myr. There doth.

Sar.   I know there doth, but not its name ;
What is it?

Myr.   In my native land a God,
And in my heart a feeling like a God's, .
Exalted ; yet I own 'tis only mortal ;
For what I feel is humble, and yet happy—
That is, it would be happy ; but——

                              [MYRRHA *pauses.*

Sar.   There comes
For ever something between us and what
We deem our happiness : let me remove
The barrier which that hesitating accent
Proclaims to thine, and mine is seal'd.

Myr.   My lord !—

Sar. My lord—my king—sire—sovereign ! thus
          it is—
For ever thus, address'd with awe. I ne'er
Can see a smile, unless in some broad banquet's
Intoxicating glare, when the buffoons
Have gorged themselves up to equality,
Or I have quaff'd me down to their abasement.
Myrrha, I can hear all these things, these names,

Lord—king—sire—monarch—nay, time was I prized
      them,
That is, I suffer'd them—from slaves and nobles;
But when they falter from the lips I love,
The lips which have been press'd to mine, a chill
Comes o'er my heart, a cold sense of the falsehood
Of this my station, which represses feeling
In those for whom I have felt most, and makes me
Wish that I could lay down the dull tiara,
And share a cottage on the Caucasus
With thee, and wear no crowns but those of flowers.

    Myr. Would that we could!

    Sar.   And dost *thou* feel this?—Why?

    Myr. Then thou wouldst know what thou canst
       never know.

    Sar. And that is——

    Myr.   The true value of a heart;
At least, a woman's.

    Sar.   I have proved a thousand—
A thousand, and a thousand.

    Myr.   Hearts?

    Sar.   I think so.

    Myr. Not one! the time may come thou may'st.

    Sar.   It will.

Hear, Myrrha; Salemenes has declared—
Or why or how he hath divined it, Belus,
Who founded our great realm, knows more than I—
But Salemenes hath declared my throne
In peril.

   Myr.   He did well.

   Sar.   And say'st *thou* so?
Thou whom he spurn'd so harshly, and now dared
Drive from our presence with his savage jeers,
And made thee weep and blush?

   Myr.   I should do both
More frequently, and he did well to call me
Back to my duty.   But thou spakest of peril—
Peril to thee——

   Sar.   Ay, from dark plots and snares
From Medes—and discontented troops and nations.
I know not what—a labyrinth of things—
A maze of mutter'd threats and mysteries:
Thou know'st the man—it is his usual custom.
But he is honest.   Come, we'll think no more on 't—
But of the midnight festival.

   Myr.   'Tis time
To think of aught save festivals.   Thou hast not
Spurn'd his sage cautions?

Sar.   What?—and dost thou fear?

Myr. Fear!—I 'm a Greek, and how should I fear
    death?

A slave, and wherefore should I dread my freedom?

  Sar. Then wherefore dost thou turn so pale?

  Myr.   I love.

  Sar. And do not I? I love thee far—far more ·

Than either the brief life or the wide realm,

Which, it may be, are menaced;—yet I blench not.

  Myr. That means thou lovest nor thyself nor me;

For he who loves another loves himself,

Even for that other's sake. This is too rash:

Kingdoms and lives are not to be so lost.

  Sar. Lost!—why, who is the aspiring chief who
    dared

Assume to win them?

  Myr.   Who is he should dread

To try so much? When he who is their ruler

Forgets himself, will they remember him?

  Sar. Myrrha!

  Myr.   Frown not upon me: you have smiled

Too often on me not to make those frowns

Bitterer to bear than any punishment

Which they may augur.—King, I am your subject!

Master, I am your slave! Man, I have loved you!—
Loved you, I know not by what fatal weakness,
Although a Greek, and born a foe to monarchs—
A slave, and hating fetters—an Ionian,
And, therefore, when I love a stranger, more
Degraded by that passion than by chains!
Still I have loved you. If that love were strong
Enough to overcome all former nature,
Shall it not claim the privilege to save you?

    Sar. *Save* me, my beauty! Thou art very fair,
And what I seek of thee is love—not safety.

    Myr. And without love where dwells security?

    Sar. I speak of woman's love.

    Myr.   The very first
Of human life must spring from woman's breast,
Your first small words are taught you from her lips,
Your first tears quench'd by her, and your last sighs
Too often breathed out in a woman's hearing,
When men have shrunk from the ignoble care
Of watching the last hour of him who led them.

    Sar. My eloquent Ionian! thou speak'st music,
The very chorus of the tragic song
I have heard thee talk of as the favourite pastime
Of thy far father-land. Nay, weep not—calm thee.

Myr. I weep not.—But I pray thee, do not speak
About my fathers or their land.

    Sar.   Yet oft
Thou speakest of them.

    Myr.   True—true: constant thought
Will overflow in words unconsciously;
But when another speaks of Greece, it wounds me.

    Sar. Well, then, how wouldst thou *save* me, as
             thou saidst?

    Myr. By teaching thee to save thyself, and not
Thyself alone, but these vast realms, from all
The rage of the worst war—the war of brethren.

    Sar. Why, child, I loathe all war, and warriors;
I live in peace and pleasure: what can man
Do more?

    Myr.   Alas! my lord, with common men
There needs too oft the show of war to keep
The substance of sweet peace; and for a king,
'Tis sometimes better to be fear'd than loved.

    Sar. And I have never sought but for the last.

    Myr. And now art neither.

    Sar.   Dost *thou* say so, Myrrha?

    Myr. I speak of civic popular love, *self* love,
Which means that men are kept in awe and law,

†

Yet not oppress'd—at least they must not think so;
Or if they think so, deem it necessary,
To ward off worse oppression, their own passions.
A king of feasts, and flowers, and wine, and revel,
And love, and mirth, was never king of glory.
      Sar. Glory! what's that?
      Myr.   Ask of the gods thy fathers.
      Sar. They cannot answer; when the priests speak
          for them,
'Tis for some small addition to the temple.
      Myr. Look to the annals of thine empire's founders.
      Sar. They are so blotted o'er with blood, I cannot.
But what wouldst have ? the empire *has been* founded.
I cannot go on multiplying empires.
      Myr. Preserve thine own.
      Sar.   At least I will enjoy it·
Come, Myrrha, let us on to the Euphrates ;
The hour invites, the galley is prepared,
And the pavilion, deck'd for our return,
In fit adornment for the evening banquet,
Shall blaze with beauty and with light, until
It seems unto the stars which are above us
Itself an opposite star; and we will sit
Crown'd with fresh flowers like ——

Myr.   Victims.

    Sar.   No, like sovereigns,

The shepherd kings of patriarchal times,

Who knew no brighter gems than summer wreaths,

And none but tearless triumphs. Let us on.

Enter PANIA.

    Pan. May the king live for ever!

    Sar.   Not an hour

Longer than he can love. How my soul hates

This language which makes life itself a lie,

Flattering dust with eternity. Well, Pania!

Be brief.

    Pan.   I am charged by Salemenes to

Reiterate his prayer unto the king,

That for this day, at least, he will not quit

The palace: when the general returns,

He will adduce such reasons as will warrant

His daring, and perhaps obtain the pardon

Of his presumption.

    Sar.   What! am I then coop'd?

Already captive? can I not even breathe

The breath of heaven? Tell prince Salemenes,

Were all Assyria raging round the walls
In mutinous myriads, I would still go forth.

   Pan. I must obey, and yet—

   Myr.   Oh, monarch, listen.—

How many a day and moon thou hast reclined
Within these palace walls in silken dalliance,
And never shown thee to thy people's longing;
Leaving thy subjects' eyes ungratified,
The satraps uncontroll'd, the gods unworshipp'd,
And all things in the anarchy of sloth, ·
'Till all, save evil, slumber'd through the realm!
And wilt thou not now tarry for a day,
A day which may redeem thee? Wilt thou not
Yield to the few still faithful a few hours,
For them, for thee, for thy past fathers' race,
And for thy sons' inheritance?

   Pan.   'Tis true!

From the deep urgency with which the prince
Despatch'd me to your sacred presence, I
Must dare to add my feeble voice to that
Which now has spoken.

   Sar.   No, it must not be.

   Myr. For the sake of thy realm!

 Sar.   Away!

 Pan.   For that
Of all thy faithful subjects, who will rally
Round thee and thine.

 Sar.   These are mere phantasies;
There is no peril:—'tis a sullen scheme
Of Salemenes, to approve his zeal,
And show himself more necessary to us.

 Myr. By all that's good and glorious take this
   counsel

 Sar. Business to-morrow.

 Myr.   Ay, or death to-night.

 Sar. Why let it come then unexpectedly,
'Midst joy and gentleness, and mirth and love;
So let me fall like the pluck'd rose!—far better
Thus than be wither'd.

 Myr.   Then thou wilt not yield,
Even for the sake of all that ever stirr'd
A monarch into action, to forego
A trifling revel.

 Sar.   No.

 Myr.   Then yield for *mine;*
For my sake!

Sar.   Thine, my Myrrha?

Myr.   'Tis the first
Boon which I e'er ask'd Assyria's king.

    Sar. That's true, and wer't my kingdom must be
        granted.   ·

Well, for thy sake, I yield me. Pania, hence!
Thou hear'st me.

    Pan.   And obey.   [*Exit* PANIA.

    Sar.   I marvel at thee.
What is thy motive, Myrrha, thus to urge me?

    Myr. Thy safety; and the certainty that nought
Could urge the prince thy kinsman to require
Thus much from thee, but some impending danger.

    Sar. And if I do not dread it; why shouldst thou?

    Myr. Because *thou* dost not fear, I fear for *thee.*

    Sar. To-morrow thou wilt smile at these vain
        fancies.

    Myr. If the worst come, I shall be where none
        weep,
And that is better than the power to smile.
And thou?

    Sar.   I shall be king, as heretofore.

    Myr. Where?

    Sar.   With Baal, Nimrod, and Semiramis,

Sole in Assyria, or with them elsewhere.
Fate made me what I am—may make me nothing—
But either that or nothing must I be;
¶ I will not live degraded.

    Myr.   Hadst thou felt
Thus always, none would ever dare degrade thee.

    Sar. And who will do so now?

    Myr.   Dost thou suspect none?

    Sar. Suspect!—that's a spy's office. Oh! we lose
Ten thousand precious moments in vain words,
And vainer fears. Within there!—Ye slaves, deck
The hall of Nimrod for the evening revel :
If I must make a prison of our palace,
At least we'll wear our fetters jocundly;
If the Euphrates be forbid us, and
The summer dwelling on its beauteous border,
Here we are still unmenaced. Ho! within there!

                  [*Exit* SARDANAPALUS.

    Myr. (*solus*). Why do I love this man? My country's
        daughters
Love none but heroes. But I have no country!
The slave hath lost all save her bonds. I love him;
And that's the heaviest link of the long chain—
To love whom we esteem not.   Be it so:

The hour is coming when he 'll need all love,
And find none. To fall from him now were baser
Than to have stabb'd him on his throne when highest
Would have been noble in my country's creed;
I was not made for either.   Could I save him,
I should not love *him* better, but myself;
And I have need of the last, for I have fallen
In my own thoughts, by loving this soft stranger:
And yet methinks I love him more, perceiving
That he is hated of his own barbarians,
The natural foes of all the blood of Greece.
Could I but wake a single thought like those
Which even the Phrygians felt when battling long
'Twixt Ilion and the sea, within his heart,
He would tread down the barbarous crowds, and
            triumph.
He loves me, and I love him; the slave loves
Her master, and would free him from his vices.
If not, I have a means of freedom still,
And if I cannot teach him how to reign,
May show him how alone a king can leave
His throne. I must not lose him from my sight.
                              [*Exit.*

ACT II. SCENE I.

The Portal of the same Hall of the Palace.

Beleses (solus). The sun goes down : methinks he
    sets more slowly,
Taking his last look of Assyria's empire.
How red he glares amongst those deepening clouds,
Like the blood he predicts. If not in vain,
Thou sun that sinkest, and ye stars which rise,
I have outwatch'd ye, reading ray by ray
The edicts of your orbs, which make Time tremble
For what he brings the nations, 'tis the furthest
Hour of Assyria's years. And yet how calm !
An earthquake should announce so great a fall—
A summer's sun discloses it. Yon disk,
To the star-read Chaldean, bears upon
Its everlasting page the end of what
Seem'd everlasting; but oh ! thou true sun !
The burning oracle of all that live,
As fountain of all life, and symbol of
Him who bestows it, wherefore dost thou limit

Thy lore unto calamity? Why not
Unfold the rise of days more worthy thine
All-glorious burst from ocean? why not dart
A beam of hope athwart the future years,
As of wrath to its days? Hear me! oh! hear me!
I am thy worshipper, thy priest, thy servant—
I have gazed on thee at thy rise and fall,
And bow'd my head beneath thy mid-day beams,
When my eye dared not meet thee. I have watch'd
For thee, and after thee, and pray'd to thee,
And sacrificed to thee, and read, and fear'd thee,
And ask'd of thee, and thou hast answer'd—but
Only to thus much: while I speak, he sinks—
Is gone—and leaves his beauty, not his knowledge,
To the delighted west, which revels in
Its hues of dying glory. Yet what is
Death, so it be but glorious? 'Tis a sunset;
And mortals may be happy to resemble
The gods but in decay.

        Enter ARBACES, *by an inner door.*

  Arb.   Beleses, why
So rapt in thy devotions? Dost thou stand

Gazing to trace thy disappearing god
Into some realm of undiscover'd day?
Our business is with night—'tis come.

    Bel.   But not
Gone.

    Arb.   Let it roll on—we are ready.

    Bel.   Yes.
Would it were over!

    Arb.   Does the Prophet doubt,
To whom the very stars shine victory?

    Bel. I do not doubt of victory—but the victor.

    Arb. Well, let thy science settle that. Meantime,
I have prepared as many glittering spears
As will out-sparkle our allies—your planets.
There is no more to thwart us. The she-king,
That less than woman, is even now upon
The waters with his female mates. The order
Is issued for the feast in the pavilion.
The first cup which he drains will be the last
Quaff'd by the line of Nimrod.

    Bel.   'Twas a brave one.

    Arb. And is a weak one—'tis worn out—we 'll
        mend it.

Bel. Art sure of that?

Arb.   Its founder was a hunter—
I am a soldier—what is there to fear?

Bel. The soldier.

Arb.   And the priest, it may be; but
If you thought thus, or think, why not retain
Your king of concubines? why stir me up?
Why spur me to this enterprise? your own
No less than mine?

Bel.   Look to the sky!

Arb.   .   I look.

Bel. What seest thou?

Arb.   A fair summer's twilight, and
The gathering of the stars.

Bel.   And midst them, mark
Yon earliest, and the brightest, which so quivers,
As it would quit its place in the blue ether.

Arb. Well?

Bel. 'Tis thy natal ruler—thy birth planet.

Arb. (touching his scabbard). My star is in this
          scabbard: when it shines,
It shall out-dazzle comets. Let us think
Of what is to be done to justify
Thy planets and their portents. When we conquer,

They shall have temples—ay, and priests—and thou
Shalt be the pontiff of—what gods thou wilt;
For I observe that they are ever just,
And own the bravest for the most devout.

   Bel. Ay, and the most devout for brave—thou hast
       not
Seen me turn back from battle.

   Arb.   No; I own thee
As firm in fight as Babylonia's captain,
As skilful in Chaldea's worship; now,
Will it but please thee to forget the priest,
And be the warrior?

   Bel.   Why not both?

   Arb.   The better;
And yet it almost shames me, we shall have
So little to effect. This woman's warfare
Degrades the very conqueror. To have pluck'd
A bold and bloody despot from his throne,
And grappled with him, clashing steel with steel,
That were heroic or to win or fall;
But to upraise my sword against this silkworm,
And hear him whine, it may be——

   Bel.   Do not deem it:
He has that in him which may make you strife yet;

And were he all you think, his guards are hardy,
And headed by the cool, stern Salemenes.

   Arb. They'll not resist.

   Bel.   Why not? they are soldiers.

   Arb.   True,
And therefore need a soldier to command them.

   Bel. That Salemenes is.

   Arb.   But not their king.
Besides, he hates the effeminate thing that governs,
For the queen's sake, his sister. Mark you not
He keeps aloof from all the revels?

   Bel.   But
Not from the council—there he is ever constant.

   Arb. And ever thwarted; what would you have
      more
To make a rebel out of? A fool reigning,
His blood dishonour'd, and himself disdain'd;
Why, it is *his* revenge we work for.

   Bel.   Could
He but be brought to think so: this, I doubt of.

   Arb. What, if we sound him?

   Bel.   Yes—if the time served.

E

Enter BALEA.

Bal. Satraps! The king commands your pre-
    sence at
The feast to-night.

   Bel.   To hear is to obey.
In the pavilion?

   Bal.   No; here in the palace.

   Arb. How! in the palace? it was not thus order'd.

   Bal. It is so order'd now.

   Arb.   And why?

   Bal.   I know not.
May I retire?

   Arb.   Stay.

   Bel. (*to Arb. aside*). Hush! let him go his way.
(*Alternately to Bal.*) Yes, Balea, thank the monarch,
    kiss the hem
Of his imperial robe, and say, his slaves
Will take the crums he deigns to scatter from
His royal table at the hour—was 't midnight?

   Bal. It was: the place, the Hall of Nimrod. Lords,
I humble me before you, and depart. [*Exit* BALEA.

Arb. I like not this same sudden change of place ;
There is some mystery: wherefore should he change
          it ?

Bel. Doth he not change a thousand times a day?
Sloth is of all things the most fanciful—
And moves more parasangs in its intents
Than generals in their marches when they seek
To leave their foe at fault.—Why dost thou muse?

Arb. He loved that gay pavilion,— it was ever
His summer dotage.

Bel. ·   And he loved his queen—
And thrice a thousand harlotry besides—
And he has loved all things by turns, except
Wisdom and glory.

Arb.   Still—I like it not.
If he has changed—why so must we : the attack
Were easy in the isolated bower,
Beset with drowsy guards and drunken courtiers ;
But in the Hall of Nimrod——

Bel.   Is it so?
Methought the haughty soldier fear'd to mount
A throne too easily—does it disappoint thee
To find there is a slipperier step or two
Than what was counted on?

                                        E 2

Arb.   When the hour comes,
Thou shalt perceive how far I fear or no.
Thou hast seen my life at stake—and gaily play'd
        for—
But here is more upon the die—a kingdom.

Bel. I have foretold already—thou wilt win it:
Then on, and prosper.

Arb.   Now were I a soothsayer,
I would have boded so much to myself.
But be the stars obey'd—I cannot quarrel
With them, nor their interpreter. Who's here?

Enter SALEMENES.

Sal. Satraps!

Bel.   My prince!

Sal.   ,   Well met—I sought ye both,
But elsewhere than the palace.

Arb.   Wherefore so?

Sal. 'Tis not the hour.

Arb.   The hour!—what hour?

Sal.   .   Of midnight.

Bel. Midnight, my lord!

Sal.   What, are you not invited?

Bel. Oh! yes—we had forgotten.

Sal.   Is it usual
Thus to forget a sovereign's invitation?

Arb. Why—we but now received it.

Sal.   Then why here?

Arb. On duty.

Sal.   On what duty?

Bel.   On the state's.
We have the privilege to approach the presence;
But found the monarch absent.

Sal. ·   And I too
Am upon duty.

Arb.   May we crave its purport?

Sal. To arrest two traitors. Guards! Within
           there!

Enter Guards.

Sal. (*continuing*).   Satraps,
Your swords.

Bel. (*delivering his*). My lord, behold my sci-
           mitar.

Arb. (*drawing his sword*). Take mine.

Sal. (*advancing*).   I will.

  Arb.   But in your heart the blade—
The hilt quits not this hand.
  Sal. (*drawing*).   How! dost thou brave me?
'Tis well—this saves a trial, and false mercy.
Soldiers, hew down the rebel!
  Arb.   Soldiers! Ay—
Alone you dare not.
  Sal.   Alone! foolish slave—
What is there in thee that a prince should shrink
   from
Of open force? We dread thy treason, not
Thy strength: thy tooth is nought without its
   venom—
The serpent's, not the lion's. Cut him down.
  Bel. (*interposing*). Arbaces! are you mad? Have
   I not render'd
My sword? Then trust like me our sovereign's
   justice.
  Arb. No—I will sooner trust the stars thou
   prat'st of
And this slight arm, and die a king at least
Of my own breath and body—so far that
None else shall chain them.

Sal. '(*to the Guards*). You hear *him*, and *me*.
Take him not,—kill.

    [*The Guards attack* ARBACES, *who defends*
       himself valiantly and dexterously till they
       waver.

Sal.   Is it even so; and must
I do the hangman's office? Recreants! see
How you should fell a traitor.

              [SALEMENES *attacks* ARBACES.

    Enter SARDANAPALUS *and Train.*

Sar.   Hold your hands—
Upon your lives, I say. What, deaf or drunken?
My sword! Oh fool, I wear no sword: here, fellow,
Give me thy weapon. ·   [*To a Guard.*

    [SARDANAPALUS *snatches a sword from one of*
       the soldiers, and makes between the combatants
       —*they separate.*

Sar.   In my very palace!
What hinders me from cleaving you in twain,
Audacious brawlers?

Bel.   Sire, your justice.

Sal.   Or—

Your weakness.

   Sar. (*raising the sword*). How?

   Sal.   Strike! so the blow's repeated

Upon yon traitor—whom you spare a moment,

I trust, for torture—I'm content.

   Sar. .   What—him!

Who dares assail Arbaces?

   Sal.   I!

   Sar.   Indeed!

Prince, you forget yourself. Upon what warrant?

   Sal. (*showing the signet*). Thine.

   Arb. (*confused*).   The king's!

   Sal.   Yes! and let the king confirm it.

   Sar. I parted not from this for such a purpose.

   Sal. You parted with it for your safety—I

Employ'd it for the best. Pronounce in person.

Here I am but your slave—a moment past

I was your representative.

   Sar.   Then sheathe

Your swords.

     [ARBACES *and* SALEMENES *return their swords*

      to the scabbards.

Sal. Mine's sheathed: I pray you sheathe *not*
      yours;
'Tis the sole sceptre left you now with safety.

Sar. A heavy one; the hilt, too, hurts my hand.
(*To a Guard*). Here, fellow, take thy weapon back.
      Well, sirs,
What doth this mean?

Bel.   The prince must answer that.

Sal. Truth upon my part, treason upon theirs.

Sar. Treason—Arbaces! treachery and Beleses!
That were an union I will not believe.

Bel. Where is the proof?

Sal.   I'll answer that, if once
The king demands your fellow-traitor's sword.

Arb. (*to Sal.*). A sword which hath been drawn as
      oft as thine
Against his foes.

Sal.   And now against his brother,
And in an hour or so against himself.

Sar. That is not possible: he dared not; no—
No—I'll not hear of such things. These vain
      bickerings
Are spawn'd in courts by base intrigues and baser

Hirelings, who live by lies on good men's lives.
You must have been deceived, my brother.

   Sal.   First
Let him deliver up his weapon, and
Proclaim himself your subject by that duty,
And I will answer all.

   Sar.   Why, if I thought so—
But no, it cannot be; the Mede Arbaces—
The trusty, rough, true soldier—the best captain
Of all who discipline our nations——No,
I 'll not insult him thus, to bid him render
The scimitar to me he never yielded
Unto our enemies. Chief, keep your weapon.

   Sal. (*delivering back the signet*). Monarch, take
       back your signet.

   Sar.   No, retain it ;
But use it with more moderation.

   Sal.   Sire,
I used it for your honour, and restore it
Because I cannot keep it with my own.
Bestow it on Arbaces.

   Sar.   So I should :
He never ask'd it.

Sal.   Doubt not, he will have it
Without that hollow semblance of respect.

    Bel. I know not what hath prejudiced the prince
So strongly 'gainst two subjects, than whom none
Have been more zealous for Assyria's weal.

    Sal. Peace, factious priest and faithless soldier!
       thou
Unit'st in thy own person the worst vices
Of the most dangerous orders of mankind.
Keep thy smooth words and juggling homilies
For those who know thee not. Thy fellow's sin
Is, at the least, a bold one, and not temper'd
By the tricks taught thee in Chaldea.

    Bel.   Hear him,
My liege—the son of Belus! he blasphemes
The worship of the land, which bows the knee
Before your fathers.

    Sar.   Oh! for that I pray you
Let him have absolution. I dispense with
The worship of dead men; feeling that I
Am mortal, and believing that the race
From whence I sprung are—what I see them—
       ashes.

Bel. King! Do not deem so: they are with the
          stars,
And——

   Sar. You shall join them there ere they will
          rise,
If you preach farther.—Why, *this* is rank treason.

   Sal. My lord!

   Sar.   To school me in the worship of
Assyria's idols! Let him be released—
Give him his sword.

   Sal.   My lord, and king, and brother,
I pray ye pause.

   Sar.   Yes, and be sermonized,
And dinn'd, and deafen'd with dead men and Baal,
And all Chaldea's starry mysteries.

   Bel. Monarch! respect them.

   Sar.   Oh! for that—I love them;
I love to watch them in the deep blue vault,
And to compare them with my Myrrha's eyes;
I love to see their rays redoubled in
The tremulous silver of Euphrates' wave,
As the light breeze of midnight crisps the broad
And rolling water, sighing through the sedges

Which fringe his banks: but whether they may be
Gods, as some say, or the abodes of gods,
As others hold, or simply lamps of night,
Worlds, or the lights of worlds, I know nor care
          not.
There's something sweet in my uncertainty
I would not change for your Chaldean lore;
Besides, I know of these all clay can know
Of aught above it, or below it—nothing.
I see their brilliancy and feel their beauty—
When they shine on my grave I shall know neither.
   Bel. For *neither,* sire, say *better.*
   Sar.   I will wait,
If it so please you, pontiff, for that knowledge.
In the mean time receive your sword, and know
That I prefer your service militant
Unto your ministry—not loving either.
   Sal. (*aside*). His lusts have made him mad. Then
          must I save him
Spite of himself.
   Sar.   Please you to hear me, Satraps!
And chiefly thou, my priest, because I doubt thee
More than the soldier; and would doubt thee all

Wert thou not half a warrior: let us part
In peace—I 'll not say pardon—which must be
Earn'd by the guilty; this I 'll not pronounce ye,
Although upon this breath of mine depends
Your own; and, deadlier for ye, on my fears.
But fear not—for that I am soft, not fearful—
And so live on. Were I the thing some think me,
Your heads would now be dripping the last drops
Of their attainted gore from the high gates
Of this our palace into the dry dust,
Their only portion of the coveted kingdom
They would be crown'd to reign o'er—let that pass.
As I have said, I will not *deem* ye guilty,
Nor *doom* ye guiltless. Albeit better men
Than ye or I stand ready to arraign you;
And should I leave your fate to sterner judges,
And proofs of all kinds, I might sacrifice
Two men, who, whatsoe'er they now are, were
Once honest. Ye are free, sirs.

    Arb.   Sire, this clemency——

    Bel. (*interrupting him*). Is worthy of yourself; and,
        although innocent,

We thank——

Sar. Priest! keep your thanksgivings for Belus;
His offspring needs none.

　　Bel.　　　　　　　　But, being innocent——

Sar. Be silent—Guilt is loud. If ye are loyal,
Ye are injured men, and should be sad, not grate-
　　ful.

　　Bel. So we should be, were justice always done
By earthly power omnipotent; but innocence
Must oft receive her right as a mere favour.

　　Sar. That's a good sentence for a homily,
Though not for this occasion. Prithee keep it
To plead thy sovereign's cause before his people.

　　Bel. I trust there is no cause.

　　Sar.　　　　　　　　No *cause,* perhaps;
But many causers:—if ye meet with such
In the exercise of your inquisitive function
On earth, or should you read of it in heaven
In some mysterious twinkle of the stars,
Which are your chronicles, I pray you note,
That there are worse things betwixt earth and
　　　　heaven
Than him who ruleth many and slays none;
And, hating not himself, yet loves his fellows

Enough to spare even those who would not spare
      him
Were they once masters—but that's doubtful. Sa-
      traps!
Your swords and persons are at liberty
To use them as ye will—but from this hour
I have no call for either. Salemenes!
Follow me.

      [*Exeunt* SARDANAPALUS, SALEMENES, *and the*
         Train, &c. leaving ARBACES *and* BELESES.

Arb.   Beleses!

Bel.   Now, what think you?

Arb. That we are lost.

Bel.   That we have won the kingdom.

Arb. What? thus suspected—with the sword slung
      o'er us
But by a single hair, and that still wavering
To be blown down by his imperious breath,
Which spared us—why, I know not.

    Bel.   Seek not why;
But let us profit by the interval.
The hour is still our own—our power the same—
The night the same we destined. He hath changed

Nothing except our ignorance of all
Suspicion into such a certainty
As must make madness of delay.

  Arb.   And yet——

  Bel. What, doubting still?

  Arb.   He spared our lives, nay, more,
Saved them from Salemenes.

  Bel.   And how long
Will he so spare? till the first drunken minute.

  Arb. Or sober, rather. Yet he did it nobly;
Gave royally what we had forfeited
Basely——

  Bel. Say bravely.

  Arb.   Somewhat of both, perhaps.
But it has touch'd me, and, whate'er betide,
I will no further on.

  Bel.   And lose the world!

  Arb. Lose any thing except my own esteem.

  Bel. I blush that we should owe our lives to
     such
A king of distaffs!

  Arb.   But no less we owe them;
And I should blush far more to take the grantor's!

Bel. Thou may'st endure whate'er thou wilt, the stars
Have written otherwise.

Arb.   Though they came down,
And marshall'd me the way in all their brightness,
I would not follow.

Bel.   This is weakness—worse
Than a scared beldam's dreaming of the dead,
And waking in the dark.—Go to—go to.

Arb. Methought he look'd like Nimrod as he spoke,
Even as the proud imperial statue stands
Looking the monarch of the kings around it,
And sways, while they but ornament, the temple.

Bel. I told you that you had too much despised him,   .
And that there was some royalty within him—
What then? he is the nobler foe.

Arb.   But we
The meaner:—Would he had not spared us!

Bel.   So—
Wouldst thou be sacrificed thus readily?

Arb. No—but it had been better to have died
Than live ungrateful.

Bel.   Oh, the souls of some men!
Thou wouldst digest what some call treason, and
Fools treachery—and, behold, upon the sudden,
Because for something or for nothing, this
Rash reveller steps, ostentatiously,
Twixt thee and Salemenes, thou art turn'd
Into—what shall I say?—Sardanapalus!
I know no name more ignominious.

    Arb.   But
An hour ago, who dared to term me such
Had held his life but lightly—as it is,
I must forgive you, even as he forgave us—
Semiramis herself would not have done it.

    Bel. No—the queen liked no sharers of the king-
        dom,
Not even a husband.

    Arb.   I must serve him truly——
    Bel. And humbly?

    Arb.   No, sir, proudly—being honest.
I shall be nearer thrones than you to heaven;
And if not quite so haughty, yet more lofty.
You may do your own deeming—you have codes,
And mysteries, and corollaries of

                          F 2

Right and wrong, which I lack for my direction,
And must pursue but what a plain heart teaches.
And now you know me.

    Bel.   Have you finish'd?

    Arb.   Yes—
With you.

    Bel.   And would, perhaps, betray as well
As quit me?

    Arb.   That's a sacerdotal thought,
And not a soldier's.

    Bel.   Be it what you will—
Truce with these wranglings, and but hear me.

    Arb.   No—
There is more peril in your subtlespirit
Than in a phalanx.

    Bel.   If it must be so—
I 'll on alone.

    Arb.   Alone!

    Bel.   Thrones hold but one.

    Arb. But this is fill'd.

    Bel.   With worse than vacancy—
A despised monarch. Look to it, Arbaces:
I have still aided, cherish'd, loved, and urged you;

Was willing even to serve you, in the hope
To serve and save Assyria: Heaven itself
Seem'd to consent, and all events were friendly,
Even to the last, till that your spirit shrunk
Into a shallow softness; but now, rather
Than see my country languish, I will be
Her saviour or the victim of her tyrant,
Or one or both, for sometimes both are one;
And, if I win, Arbaces is my servant.

 Arb. Your servant!

 Bel.   Why not? better than be slave,
The *pardon'd* slave of *she* Sardanapalus.

     Enter PANIA.

 Pan. My lords, I bear an order from the king.

 Arb. It is obey'd ere spoken.

 Bel.   Notwithstanding,
Let's hear it.

 Pan. Forthwith, on this very night,
Repair to your respective satrapies
Of Babylon and Media.

 Bel.   With our troops?

Pan. My order is unto the satraps and
Their household train.

 Arb.   But——

 Bel.   It must be obey'd;
Say, we depart.

 Pan.   My order is to see you
Depart, and not to bear your answer.

 Bel. (aside).   Ay!
Well, sir, we will accompany you hence.

 Pan. I will retire to marshal forth the guard
Of honour which befits your rank, and wait
Your leisure, so that it the hour exceeds not.

          [*Exit* PANIA.

 Bel. Now then obey!

 Arb.   Doubtless.

 Bel.   Yes, to the gates
That grate the palace, which is now our prison,
No further.

 Arb. Thou hast harp'd the truth indeed!
The realm itself, in all its wide extension,
Yawns dungeons at each step for thee and me.

 Bel. Graves!

 Arb. If I thought so, this good sword should dig
One more than mine.

 Bel.   It shall have work enough:
Let me hope better than thou augurest;
At present let us hence as best we may.
Thou dost agree with me in understanding
This order as a sentence?

 Arb.   Why, what other
Interpretation should it bear? it is
The very policy of orient monarchs—
Pardon and poison—favours and a sword—
A distant voyage, and an eternal sleep.
How many satraps in his father's time—
For he I own is, or at least *was*, bloodless—

 Bel. But *will* not, *can* not be so now.

 Arb.   I doubt it.
How many satraps have I seen set out
In his sire's day for mighty vice-royalties,
Whose tombs are on their path! I know not how,
But they all sicken'd by the way, it was
So long and heavy.

 Bel.   Let us but regain
The free air of the city, and we'll shorten
The journey.

 Arb. 'Twill be shorten'd at the gates,
It may be.

Bel.   No; they hardly will risk that.
They mean us to die privately, but not
Within the palace or the city walls,
Where we are known and may have partisans:
If they had meant to slay us here, we were
No longer with the living. Let us hence.

 Arb. If I but thought he did not mean my
   life——

 Bel. Fool! hence—what else should despotism
   alarm'd

Mean? Let us but rejoin our troops, and march.

 Arb. Towards our provinces?

 Bel.   No; towards your kingdom.
There's time, there's heart, and hope, and power, and
   means,
Which their half measures leave us in full scope.—
Away!

 Arb. And I even yet repenting must
Relapse to guilt!

 Bel.   Self-defence is a virtue,
Sole bulwark of all right. Away, I say!
Let's leave this place, the air grows thick and
   choking,
And the walls have a scent of night-shade—hence!

Let us not leave them time for further council.
Our quick departure proves our civic zeal;
Our quick departure hinders our good escort,
The worthy Pania, from anticipating
The orders of some parasangs from hence;
Nay, there's no other choice but——hence, I say.

       [*Exit with* ARBACES, *who follows reluctantly.*

    Enter SARDANAPALUS *and* SALEMENES.

  Sar. Well, all is remedied and without blood-
      shed,
That worst of mockeries of a remedy;
We are now secure by these men's exile.
  Sal.   Yes,
As he who treads on flowers is from the adder
Twined round their roots.
  Sar.   Why, what wouldst have me do?
  Sal. Undo what you have done.
  Sar.   Revoke my pardon?
  Sal. Replace the crown now tottering on your
      temples.
  Sar. That were tyrannical.
  Sal.   But sure.

Sar.   We are so.
What danger can they work upon the frontier?

  Sal. They are not there yet—never should they
      be so,
Were I well listen'd to.

  Sar.   Nay, I *have* listen'd
Impartially to thee—why not to them?

  Sal. You may know that hereafter; as it is,
I take my leave, to order forth the guard.

  Sar. And you will join us at the banquet?

  Sal.   Sire,
Dispense with me—I am no wassailer:
Command me in all service save the Bacchant's.

  Sar. Nay, but 'tis fit to revel now and then.

  Sal. And fit that some should watch for those who
     revel
Too oft. Am I permitted to depart?

  Sar. Yes——Stay a moment, my good Salemenes,
My brother, my best subject, better prince
Than I am king. You should have been the mo-
     narch,
And I—I know not what, and care not; but
Think not I am insensible to all
Thine honest wisdom, and thy rough yet kind,

Though oft reproving, sufferance of my follies.
If I have spared these men against thy counsel,
That is, their lives—it is not that I doubt
The advice was sound; but, let them live: we will
          not
Cavil about their lives—so let them mend them.
Their banishment will leave me still sound sleep,
Which their death had not left me.

    Sal.   Thus you run
The risk to sleep for ever, to save traitors—
A moment's pang now changed for years of crime.
Still let them be made quiet.

    Sar.   Tempt me not:
My word is past.

    Sal.   But it may be recall'd.

    Sar. 'Tis royal.

    Sal.   And should therefore be decisive.
This half indulgence of an exile serves
But to provoke—a pardon should be full,
Or it is none.

    Sar.   And who persuaded me
After I had repeal'd them, or at least
Only dismiss'd them from our presence, who
Urged me to send them to their satrapies?

Sal. True; that I had forgotten; that is, sire,
If they e'er reach their satrapies—why, then,
Reprove me more for my advice.

　Sar.　　　　　　　　　　　And if
They do not reach them—look to it!—in safety,
In safety, mark me—and security—
Look to thine own.

　Sal.　　　　　　　Permit me to depart;
Their *safety* shall be cared for.

　Sar.　　　　　　　　　Get thee hence, then;
And, prithee, think more gently of thy brother.

　Sal. Sire, I shall ever duly serve my sovereign.
　　　　　　　　　　　　[*Exit* SALEMENES.

　Sar. (*solus*). That man is of a temper too severe:
Hard but as lofty as the rock, and free
From all the taints of common earth—while I
Am softer clay, impregnated with flowers.
But as our mould is, must the produce be.
If I have err'd this time, 'tis on the side
Where error sits most lightly on that sense,
I know not what to call it; but it reckons
With me ofttimes for pain, and sometimes plea-
　　　　　sure;
A spirit which seems placed about my heart

To court its throbs, not quicken them, and ask
Questions which mortal never dared to ask me,
Nor Baal, though an oracular deity—
Albeit his marble face majestical
Frowns as the shadows of the evening dim
His brows to changed expression, till at times
I think the statue looks in act to speak.
Away with these vain thoughts, I will be joyous—
And here comes Joy's true herald.

Enter MYRRHA.

  Myr.   King! the sky
Is overcast, and musters muttering thunder,
In clouds that seem approaching fast, and show
In forked flashes a commanding tempest.
Will you then quit the palace?
  Sar.   Tempest, sayst thou?
  Myr. Ay, my good lord.
  Sar.   For my own part, I should be
Not ill content to vary the smooth scene,
And watch the warring elements; but this
Would little suit the silken garments and

Smooth faces of our festive friends. Say, Myrrha,
Art thou of those who dread the roar of clouds?

    Myr. In my own country we respect their voices
As auguries of Jove.

    Sar.   Jove—ay, your Baal—
Ours also has a property in thunder,
And ever and anon some falling bolt
Proves his divinity, and yet sometimes
Strike his own altars.

    Myr.   That were a dread omen.

    Sar. Yes—for the priests. Well, we will not go
        forth
Beyond the palace walls to-night, but make
Our feast within.

    Myr.   Now, Jove be praised! that he
Hath heard the prayer thou wouldst not hear. The
        gods
Are kinder to thee than thou to thyself,
And flash this storm between thee and thy foes,
To shield thee from them.

    Sar.   Child, if there be peril,
Methinks it is the same within these walls
As on the river's brink.

 Myr.   Not so; these walls
Are high and strong, and guarded. Treason has
To penetrate through many a winding way,
And massy portal; but in the pavilion
There is no bulwark.
 Sar.   No, nor in the palace,
Nor in the fortress, nor upon the top
Of cloud-fenced Caucasus, where the eagle sits
Nested in pathless clefts, if treachery be:
Even as the arrow finds the airy king,
The steel will reach the earthly. But be calm:
The men, or innocent or guilty, are
Banish'd, and far upon their way.
 Myr.   They live, then?
 Sar. So sanguinary? *Thou!*
 Myr.   I would not shrink
From just infliction of due punishment
On those who seek your life: wer't otherwise,
I should not merit mine. Besides, you heard
The princely Salemenes.
 Sar.   This is strange;
The gentle and the austere are both against me,
And urge me to revenge.

Myr.   'Tis a Greek virtue.

Sar. But not a kingly one—I 'll none on 't ; or
If ever I indulge in 't, it shall be
With kings—my equals.

    Myr.   These men sought to be so.

Sar. Myrrha, this is too feminine, and springs
From fear——

    Myr.   For you.

    Sar.   No matter—still 'tis fear.
I have observed your sex, once roused to wrath,
Are timidly vindictive to a pitch
Of perseverance, which I would not copy.
I thought you were exempt from this, as from
The childish helplessness of Asian women.

    Myr. My lord, I am no boaster of my love,
Nor of my attributes ; I have shared your splen-
        dour,   .   ꜰ
And will partake your fortunes. You may live
To find one slave more true than subject myriads ;
But this the gods avert! I am content
To be beloved on trust for what I feel,
Rather than prove it to you in your griefs,
Which might not yield to any cares of mine.

Sar. Griefs cannot come where perfect love exists,
Except to heighten it, and vanish from
That which it could not scare away. Let's in—
The hour approaches, and we must prepare
To meet the invited guests, who grace our feast.

                          [*Exeunt.*

ACT III. SCENE I.

*The Hall of the Palace illuminated—*SARDANAPALUS
*and his Guests at Table—A Storm without, and
Thunder occasionally heard during the Banquet.*

Sar. Fill full! Why this is as it should be: here
Is my true realm, amidst bright eyes and faces
Happy as fair! Here sorrow cannot reach.
    Zam. Nor elsewhere—where the king is, plea-
        sure sparkles.
  Sar. Is not this better now than Nimrod's huntings,
Or my wild grandam's chase in search of kingdoms
She could not keep when conquer'd?
    Alt.   ·   Mighty though
They were, as all thy royal line have been,
Yet none of those who went before have reach'd
The acmé of Sardanapalus, who
Has placed his joy in peace—the sole true glory.

Sar. And pleasure, good Altada, to which glory
Is but the path. What is it that we seek?
Enjoyment! We have cut the way short to it,
And not gone tracking it through human ashes,
Making a grave with every footstep.

 Zam.   No;
All hearts are happy, and all voices bless
The king of peace, who holds a world in jubilee.

 Sar. Art sure of that? I have heard otherwise;
Some say that there be traitors.

 Zam.   Traitors they
Who dare to say so!—'Tis impossible.
What cause?

 Sar.   What cause? true,—fill the goblet up;
We will not think of them: there are none such,
Or if there be, they are gone.

 Alt.   Guests, to my pledge!
Down on your knees, and drink a measure to
The safety of the king—the monarch, say I?
The god Sardanapalus!

    [ZAMES *and the Guests kneel, and exclaim—*
       Mightier than

          G 2

His father Baal, the god Sardanapalus!

> [*It thunders as they kneel; some start up in confusion.*

Zam. Why do ye rise, my friends? In that strong peal
His father gods consented.

Myr.   Menaced, rather.
King, wilt thou bear this mad impiety?

Sar. Impiety!—nay, if the sires who reign'd
Before me can be gods, I 'll not disgrace
Their lineage.   But arise, my pious friends,
Hoard your devotion for the thunderer there:
I seek but to be loved, not worshipp'd.

All.   Both—
Both you must ever be by all true subjects.

Sar. Methinks the thunders still increase: it is
An awful night.

Myr.   Oh yes, for those who have
No palace to protect their worshippers.

Sar. That's true, my Myrrha; and could I con-
vert
My realm to one wide shelter for the wretched,
I 'd do it.

Myr.   Thou 'rt no god, then, not to be
Able to work a will so good and general,
As thy wish would imply.

    Sar.   And your gods, then,
Who can, and do not?

    Myr. ·   Do not speak of that,
Lest we provoke them.

    Sar.   True, they love not censure
Better than mortals. Friends, a thought has struck
       me:
Were there no temples, would there, think ye, be
Air worshippers? that is, when it is angry,
And pelting as even now.

    Myr.   The Persian prays
Upon his mountain.

    Sar.   Yes, when the sun shines.

    Myr. And I would ask if this your palace were
Unroof'd and desolate, how many flatterers
Would lick the dust in which the king lay low?

    Alt. The fair Ionian is too sarcastic
Upon a nation whom she knows not well;
The Assyrians know no pleasure but their king's,
And homage is their pride.

Sar.   Nay, pardon, guests,
The fair Greek's readiness of speech.

Alt.   Pardon! sire:
We honour her of all things next to thee.
Hark! what was that?

Zam.   That! nothing but the jar
Of distant portals shaken by the wind.

Alt. It sounded like the clash of—hark again!

Zam. The big rain pattering on the roof.

Sar.   No more.
Myrrha, my love, hast thou thy shell in order?
Sing me a song of Sappho, her, thou know'st,
Who in thy country threw——

Enter PANIA, *with his Sword and Garments bloody,
and disordered. The Guests rise in confusion.*

Pan. (*to the Guards*).   Look to the portals;
And with your best speed to the wall without.
Your arms! To arms! The king's in danger. Mon-
              arch!
Excuse this haste,—'tis faith.

Sar.   Speak on.

Pan.   It is

As Salemenes fear'd ; the faithless satrape——

   Sar. You are wounded—give some wine. Take
      breath, good Pania.

   Pan. 'Tis nothing—a mere flesh wound. I am
      worn

More with my speed to warn my sovereign,

Than hurt in his defence.

   Myr.   ·   Well, sir, the rebels.

   Pan. Soon as Arbaces and Beleses reach'd

Their stations in the city, they refused

To march; and on my attempt to use the power

Which I was delegated with, they call'd

Upon their troops, who rose in fierce defiance.

   Myr. All ?

   Pan.   Too many.

   Sar.   Spare not of thy free speech

To spare mine ears the truth.

   Pan.   My own slight guard

Were faithful, and what's left of it is still so.

   Myr. And are these all the force still faithful ?

   Pan.   No—

The Bactrians, now led on by Salemenes,

Who even then was on his way, still urged
By strong suspicion of the Median chiefs,
Are numerous, and make strong head against
The rebels, fighting inch by inch, and forming
An orb around the palace, where they mean
To centre all their force, and save the king.
(*He hesitates*).   I am charged to ——

 Myr.   'Tis no time for hesitation.

 Pan. Prince Salemenes doth implore the king
To arm himself, although but for a moment,
And show himself unto the soldiers: his
Sole presence in this instant might do more
Than hosts can do in his behalf.

 Sar.   What, ho!
My armour there.

 Myr.   And wilt thou ?

 Sar.   Will I not?
Ho, there!—But seek not for the buckler: 'tis
Too heavy:—a light cuirass and my sword.
Where are the rebels?

 Pan.   Scarce a furlong's length
From the outward wall, the fiercest conflict rages.

 Sar. Then I may charge on horseback. Sfero, ho!

Order my horse out.—There is space enough
Even in our courts, and by the outer gate,
To marshal half the horsemen of Arabia.

> [*Exit* SPERO *for the armour.*

Myr. How I do love thee !

Sar.   I ne'er doubted it.

Myr. But now I know thee.

Sar. (*to his Attendant*). Bring down my spear,
      too.—

Where 's Salemenes?

Pan.   Where a soldier should be,
In the thick of the fight.

Sar.   Then hasten to him——Is
The path still open, and communication
Left 'twixt the palace and the phalanx?

Pan.   'Twas
When I late left him, and I have no fear:
Our troops were steady, and the phalanx form'd.

Sar. Tell him to spare his person for the pre-
      sent,
And that I will not spare my own—and say,
I come.

Pan.   There 's victory in the very word.

> [*Exit* PANIA.

Sar. Altada—Zames—forth, and arm ye! There
Is all in readiness in the armoury.
See that the women are bestow'd in safety
In the remote apartments: let a guard
Be set before them, with strict charge to quit
The post but with their lives—command it, Zames.
Altada, arm yourself, and return here;
Your post is near our person.

    [*Exeunt* ZAMES, ALTADA, *and all save* MYRRHA.

Enter SFERO *and others with the King's Arms, &c.*

Sfe.   King! your armour.
Sar. (*arming himself*). Give me the cuirass—so:
    my baldric; now
My sword: I had forgot the helm, where is it?
That's well—no, 'tis too heavy: you mistake, too—
It was not this I meant, but that which bears
A diadem around it.
    Sfe.   Sire, I deem'd
That too conspicuous from the precious stones
To risk your sacred brow beneath—and, trust me,
This is of better metal, though less rich.

Sar. You deem'd! Are you too turn'd a rebel?
· Fellow!
Your part is to obey : return, and—no—
It is too late—I will go forth without it.

Sfe. At least wear this.

Sar.   Wear Caucasus! why, 'tis
A mountain on my temples.

Sfe.   Sire, the meanest
Soldier goes not forth thus exposed to battle.
All men will recognize you—for the storm
Has ceased, and the moon breaks forth in her bright-
         ness.

Sar. I go forth to be recognized, and thus
Shall be so sooner.   Now—my spear! I'm arm'd.

         [*In going stops short, and turns to* Sfero.
Sfero—I had forgotten—bring the mirror *.

Sfe. The mirror, sire?

Sar.   Yes, sir, of polish'd brass,
Brought from the spoils of India—but be speedy.

                              [*Exit* Sfero.

Sar. Myrrha, retire unto a place of safety.
Why went you not forth with the other damsels?

---

         * " Such the *mirror* Otho held
            In the Illyrian field."—See *Juvenal.*

Myr. Because my place is here.

Sar.   And when I am gone——

Myr. I follow.

Sar.   *You!* to battle?

Myr.   If it were so,
'Twere not the first Greek girl had trod the path.
I will await here your *return.*

Sar.   The place
Is spacious, and the first to be sought out,
If they prevail; and, if it should be so,
And I return not——

Myr.   Still, we meet again.

Sar. How?

Myr.   In the spot where all must meet at last—
In Hades! if there be, as I believe,
A shore beyond the Styx; and if there be not,
In ashes.

Sar.   Darest thou so much?

Myr.   I dare all things
Except survive what I have loved, to be
A rebel's booty: forth, and do your bravest.

Re-enter SFERO *with the mirror.*

Sar. (*looking at · himself*). This cuirass fits me
　　well, the baldric better,
And the helm not at all.　Methinks, I seem
　　　[*Flings away the helmet after trying it again.*
Passing well in these toys; and now to prove them.
Altada!　Where's Altada?
　　Sfe.　　　　　　　　　Waiting, sire,
Without : he has your shield in readiness.
　　Sar.　True; I forgot he is my shield-bearer
By right of blood, derived from age to age.
Myrrha, embrace me; yet once more—once more—
Love me, whate'er betide.　My chiefest glory
Shall be to make me worthier of your love.
　　Myr.　Go forth, and conquer!
　　　　　　　　　　[*Exit* SARDANAPALUS *and* SFERO.
　　　　　　　　　　　　Now, I am alone.
All are gone forth, and of that all how few
Perhaps return.　Let him but vanquish, and
Me perish!　If he vanquish not, I perish;
For I will not outlive him.　He has wound
About my heart, I know not how nor why.

Not for that he is king; for now his kingdom
Rocks underneath his throne, and the earth yawns
To yield him no more of it than a grave;
And yet I love him more.　Oh, mighty Jove!
Forgive this monstrous love for a barbarian,
Who knows not of Olympus: yes, I love him
Now, now, far more than——Hark—to the war
　　　shout!
Methinks it nears me.　If it should be so,
　　　　　　　　[*She draws forth a small vial.*
This cunning Colchian poison, which my father
Learn'd to compound on Euxine shores, and taught
　　　me
How to preserve, shall free me!　It had freed me
Long ere this hour, but that I loved, until
I half forgot I was a slave:—where all
Are slaves save one, and proud of servitude,
So they are served in turn by something lower
In the degree of bondage, we forget
That shackles worn like ornaments no less
Are chains.　Again that shout! and now the clash
Of arms—and now—and now——

Enter ALTADA.

Alt.   Ho, Sfero, ho!

Myr. He is not here; what wouldst thou with
     him? How
Goes on the conflict?

Alt.   Dubiously and fiercely.

Myr. And the king?

Alt.   Like a king. I must find Sfero,
And bring him a new spear and his own helmet.
He fights till now bare-headed, and by far
Too much exposed. The soldiers knew his face,
And the foe too; and in the moon's broad light,
His silk tiara and his flowing hair
Make him a mark too royal. Every arrow
Is pointed at the fair hair and fair features,
And the broad fillet which crowns both.

Myr.   Ye gods,
Who fulmine o'er my father's land, protect him!
Were you sent by the king?

Alt.   By Salemenes,
Who sent me privily upon this charge,

†

Without the knowledge of the careless sovereign.
The king! the king fights as he revels! ho!
What, Sfero! I will seek the armoury,
He must be there.   [*Exit* ALTADA.

    Myr.   'Tis no dishonour—no—
'Tis no dishonour to have loved this man.
I almost wish now, what I never wish'd
Before, that he were Grecian. If Alcides
Were shamed in wearing Lydian Omphale's
She-garb, and wielding.her vile distaff; surely
He, who springs up a Hercules at once,
Nursed in effeminate arts from youth to manhood,
And rushes from the banquet to the battle,
As though it were a bed of love, deserves
That a Greek girl should be his paramour,
And a Greek bard his minstrel, a Greek tomb
His monument. How goes the strife, sir?

                Enter an Officer.

    Officer.   Lost,
Lost almost past recovery. Zames! Where
Is Zames?

Myr.   Posted with the guard appointed
To watch before the apartment of the women.

          [*Exit Officer.*

  Myr. (*solus*). He's gone; and told no more than
    that all's lost!
What need have I to know more?   In those words,
Those little words, a kingdom and a king,
A line of thirteen ages, and the lives
Of thousands, and the fortune of all left
With life, are merged; and I, too, with the great,
Like a small bubble breaking with the wave
Which bore it, shall be nothing.   At the least
My fate is in my keeping: no proud victor
Shall count me with his spoils. ·

      Enter PANIA.

  Pan.   Away with me,
Myrrha, without delay; we must not lose
A moment—all that's left us now.
   Myr.   The king?
  Pan. Sent me here to conduct you hence, beyond
The river, by a secret passage.

            H

Myr.   Then
He lives——

   Pan.   And charged me to secure your life,
And beg you to live on for his sake, till
He can rejoin you.

   Myr.   Will he then give way?

   Pan. Not till the last. Still, still he does whate'er
Despair can do; and step by step disputes
The very palace.

   Myr.   They are here, then :—ay,
Their shouts come ringing through the ancient halls,
Never profaned by rebel echoes till
This fatal night. Farewell, Assyria's line!
Farewell to all of Nimrod!   Even the name
Is now no more.

   Pan.   Away with me—away!

   Myr. No! I'll die here!—Away, and tell your
          king
I loved him to the last.

Enter SARDANAPALUS *and* SALEMENES *with Soldiers.* PANIA *quits* MYRRHA, *and ranges himself with them.*

   Sar.   Since it is thus,
We'll die where we were born—in our own halls.
Serry your ranks—stand firm. I have despatch'd
A trusty satrap for the guard of Zames,
All fresh and faithful; they'll be here anon.
All is not over.—Pania, look to Myrrha.
                  [PANIA *returns towards* MYRRHA.
   Sal. We have breathing time; yet one more charge,
          my friends—
One for Assyria!
   Sar.   Rather say for Bactria!
My faithful Bactrians, I will henceforth be
King of your nation, and we'll hold together
This realm as province.
   Sal.   Hark! they come—they come.

Enter BELESES *and* ARBACES *with the Rebels.*

Arb. Set on, we have them in the toil. Charge!
          Charge!

Bel. On! on!—Heaven fights for us and with
          us.—On!

[*They charge the King and* SALEMENES *with
          their Troops, who defend themselves till the
          Arrival of* ZAMES, *with the Guard before
          mentioned. The Rebels are then driven off, and
          pursued by* SALEMENES, *&c. As the King
          is going to join the pursuit,* BELESES *crosses
          him.*

Bel. Ho! tyrant—*I* will end this war.

Sar.   Even so,
My warlike priest, and precious prophet, and
Grateful and trusty subject:—yield, I pray thee.
I would reserve thee for a fitter doom,
Rather than dip my hands in holy blood.

Bel. Thine hour is come.

Sar.   No, thine.—I 've lately read,
Though but a young astrologer, the stars;

And ranging round the zodiac, found thy fate
In the sign of the Scorpion, which proclaims
That thou wilt now be crush'd.

    Bel.   But not by thee.

  [They fight; BELESES is wounded and disarmed.
  Sar. (raising his sword to despatch him, exclaims)—
Now call upon thy planets, will they shoot
From the sky to preserve their seer and credit?

    [A Party of Rebels enter and rescue BELESES.
      They assail the King, who, in turn, is rescued
      by a Party of his Soldiers, who drive the
      Rebels off.

The villain was a prophet after all.
Upon them—ho! there—victory is ours.

                      [Exit in pursuit.

    Myr. (to Pan). Pursue! Why stand'st thou here,
        and leavest the ranks
Of fellow-soldiers conquering without thee?

    Pan. The king's command was not to quit thee.

    Myr.   *Me!*

Think not of me—a single soldier's arm
Must not be wanting now. I ask no guard,
I need no guard: what, with a world at stake,
Keep watch upon a woman? Hence, I say,

Or thou art shamed! Nay, then, *I* will go forth,
A feeble female, 'midst their desperate strife,
And bid thee guard me *there*—where thou shouldst
   shield
Thy sovereign.   *[Exit* MYRRHA.
 Pan.   Yet stay, damsel! She is gone.
If aught of ill betide her, better I
Had lost my life. Sardanapalus holds her
Far dearer than his kingdom, yet he fights
For that too; and can I do less than him,
Who never flesh'd a scimitar till now?
Myrrha, return, and I obey you, though
In disobedience to the monarch. *[Exit* PANIA.

 Enter ALTADA *and* SFERO, *by an opposite door.*

 Alt.   Myrrha!
What, gone? yet she was here when the fight raged,
And Pania also. Can aught have befallen them?
 Sfe. I saw both safe, when late the rebels fled:
They probably are but retired to make
Their way back to the harem.
 Alt.   If the king
Prove victor, as it seems even now he must,

And miss his own Ionian, we are doom'd
To worse than captive rebels.

    Sfe.   Let us trace them ;
She cannot be fled far; and, found, she makes
A richer prize to our soft sovereign
Than his recover'd kingdom.

    Alt.   Baal himself
Ne'er fought more fiercely to win empire, than
His silken son to save it: he defies
All augury of foes or friends ; and like
The close and sultry summer's day, which bodes
A twilight tempest, bursts forth in such thunder
As sweeps the air and deluges the earth.
The man 's inscrutable.

    Sfe.   Not more than others.
All are the sons of circumstance : away—
Let 's seek the slave out, or prepare to be
Tortured for his infatuation, and
Condemn'd without a crime.   [*Exeunt.*

    Enter SALEMENES *and Soldiers, &c.*

    Sal.   The triumph is

Flattering: they are beaten backward from the
    palace,
And we have open'd regular access
To the troops station'd on the other side
Euphrates, who may still be true; nay, must be,
When they hear of our victory. But where
Is the chief victor? where's the king?

Enter SARDANAPALUS, *cum suis, &c. and* MYRRHA.

  Sar.   Here, brother.
  Sal. Unhurt, I hope.
  Sar.   Not quite; but let it pass.
We've clear'd the palace——
  Sal.   And I trust the city.
Our numbers gather; and I have order'd onward
A cloud of Parthians, hitherto reserved,
All fresh and fiery, to be pour'd upon them
In their retreat, which soon will be a flight.
  Sar. It is already, or at least they march'd
Faster than I could follow with my Bactrians,
Who spared no speed. I am spent; give me a seat.
  Sal. There stands the throne, sire.

   Sar.   'Tis no place to rest on,
For mind nor body: let me have a couch,

                        [*They place a seat.*

A peasant's stool, I care not what: so—now
I breathe more freely.

   Sal.   This great hour has proved
The brightest and most glorious of your life.

    Sar. And the most tiresome. Where 's my cup-
         bearer?

Bring me some water.

    Sal. (*smiling*).   'Tis the first time he
Ever had such an order: even I,
Your most austere of counsellors, would now
Suggest a purpler beverage.

   Sar.   Blood—doubtless.

But there 's enough of that shed; as for wine,
I have learn'd to-night the price of the pure ele-
      ment:

Thrice have I drank of it, and thrice renew'd,
With greater strength than the grape ever gave me,
My charge upon the rebels. Where 's the soldier
Who gave me water in his helmet?

    One of the Guards.   Slain, sire!

An arrow pierced his brain, while, scattering
The last drops from his helm, he stood in act
To place it on his brows.

 Sar.   Slain! unrewarded!
And slain to serve my thirst: that 's hard, poor slave !
Had he but lived, I would have gorged him with
Gold: all the gold of earth could ne'er repay
The pleasure of that draught; for I was parch'd
As I am now. [*They bring water—he drinks.*
     I live again—from henceforth
The goblet I reserve for hours of love,
But war on water.

 Sal.   And that bandage, sire,
Which girds your arm?

  Sar.   A scratch from brave Beleses.

 Myr. Oh! he is wounded!

  Sar.   Not too much of that;
And yet it feels a little stiff and painful,
Now I am cooler.

 Myr.   You have bound it with——

 Sar. The fillet of my diadem: the first time
That ornament was ever aught to me
Save an incumbrance.

Myr. (*to the Attendants*). Summon speedily
A leech of the most skilful: pray, retire ;
I will unbind your wound and tend it.
　　Sar.　　　　　　　　　　　Do so,
For now it throbs sufficiently: but what
Know'st thou of wounds? yet wherefore do I ask?
Know'st thou, my brother, where I lighted on
This minion?
　　Sal.　　　Herding with the other females,
Like frighten'd antelopes.
　　Sar.　　　　　　　No : like the dam
Of the young lion, femininely raging,
(And femininely meaneth furiously,
Because all passions in excess are female),
Against the hunter flying with her cub,
She urged on with her voice and gesture, and
Her floating hair and flashing eyes, the soldiers
In the pursuit.
　　Sal.　　　Indeed!
　　Sar.　　　　　　　You see, this night
Made warriors of more than me.　I paused
To look upon her, and her kindled cheek;
Her large black eyes, that flash'd through her long
　　　　　hair

As it stream'd o'er her; her blue veins that rose
Along her most transparent brow; her nostril
Dilated from its symmetry; her lips
Apart; her voice that clove through all the din,
As a lute's pierceth through the cymbal's clash,
Jarr'd but not drown'd by the loud brattling; her
Waved arms, more dazzling with their own born
         whiteness
Than the steel her hand held, which she caught up
From a dead soldier's grasp; all these things made
Her seem unto the troops a prophetess
Of victory, or Victory herself,
Come down to hail us hers.

   Sal. (*aside*).   ·   This is too much.
Again the love-fit 's on him, and all 's lost,
Unless we turn his thoughts.

               (*Aloud.*) But pray thee, sire,
Think of your wound—you said even now 'twas
     painful.

   Sar. That 's true, too; but I must not think of it.

   Sal. I have look'd to all things needful, and will
     now
Receive reports of progress made in such

Orders as I had given, and then return
To hear your further pleasure.

   Sar.   Be it so.

   Sal. (*in retiring*). Myrrha!

   Myr.   Prince.

   Sal.   You have shown a soul to-night,
Which, were he not my sister's lord——But now
I have no time: thou lovest the king?

   Myr.   I love
Sardanapalus.

   Sal.   . But wouldst have him king still?

   Myr. I would not have him less than what he
       should be.

   Sal. Well, then, to have him king, and yours,
       and all
He should, or should not be; to have him *live*,
Let him not sink back into luxury.
You have more power upon his spirit than
Wisdom within these walls, or fierce rebellion
Raging without: look well that he relapse not.

   Myr. There needed not the voice of Salemenes
To urge me on to this: I will not fail.
All that a woman's weakness can——

   Sal   Is power

Omnipotent o'er such a heart as his;
Exert it wisely.   [*Exit* SALEMENES.

 Sar.   Myrrha! what, at whispers
With my stern brother? I shall soon be jealous.

 Myr. (*smiling*). You have cause, sire; for on the
   earth there breathes not
A man more worthy of a woman's love—
A soldier's trust—a subject's reverence—
A king's esteem—the whole world's admiration!

 Sar. Praise him, but not so warmly. I must not
Hear those sweet lips grow eloquent in aught
That throws me into shade; yet you speak truth.

 Myr. And now retire, to have your wound look'd to.
Pray, lean on me.

 Sar.   Yes, love! but not from pain.
       [*Exeunt omnes.*

ACT IV. SCENE I.

SARDANAPALUS *discovered sleeping upon a Couch and occasionally disturbed in his Slumbers, with* MYRRHA *watching.*

Myr. (*sola, gazing*). I have stolen upon his rest,
            if rest it be,
Which thus convulses slumber: shall I wake him?
No, he seems calmer. Oh, thou God of Quiet!
Whose reign is o'er seal'd eyelids and soft dreams,
Or deep, deep sleep, so as to be unfathom'd,
Look like thy brother, Death—so still—so stirless—
For then we are happiest, as it may be, we
Are happiest of all within the realm
Of thy stern, silent, and unwakening twin.
Again he moves—again the play of pain
Shoots o'er his features, as the sudden gust
Crisps the reluctant lake that lay so calm

Beneath the mountain shadow; or the blast
Ruffles the autumn leaves, that drooping cling
Faintly and motionless to their loved boughs.
I must awake him—yet not yet: who knows
From what I rouse him? It seems pain; but if
I quicken him to heavier pain? The fever
Of this tumultuous night, the grief too of
His wound, though slight, may cause all this, and
      shake
Me more to see than him to suffer. No:
Let Nature use her own maternal means,—
And I await to second not disturb her.

 Sar. (*awakening*). Not so—although ye multiplied
      the stars,
And gave them to me as a realm to share
From you and with you! I would not so purchase
The empire of eternity. Hence—hence—
Old hunter of the earliest brutes! and ye,
Who hunted fellow-creatures as if brutes;
Once bloody mortals—and now bloodier idols,
If your priests lie not! And thou, ghastly bel-
      dame!
Dripping with dusky gore, and trampling on

The carcasses of Inde—away! away!
Where am I? Where the spectres? Where——No—
    that
Is no false phantom: I should know it 'midst
All that the dead dare gloomily raise up
From their black gulf to daunt the living. Myrrha!

   Myr. Alas! thou art pale, and on thy brow the
    drops
Gather like night dew. My beloved, hush—
Calm thee. Thy speech seems of another world,
And thou art loved of this. Be of good cheer;
All will go well.

   Sar.   Thy *hand*—so—'tis thy hand;
'Tis flesh; grasp—clasp—yet closer, till I feel
Myself that which I was.

   Myr.   At least know me
For what I am, and ever must be—thine.

   Sar. I know it now. I know this life again.
Ah, Myrrha! I have been where we shall be.

   Myr. My lord!

   Sar. I've been i' the grave—where worms are lords
And kings are——But I did not deem it so;
I thought 'twas nothing.

                        I

Myr.   So it is; except
Unto the timid, who anticipate
That which may never be.

    Sar.   Oh, Myrrha! if
Sleep shows such things, what may not death dis-
        close?

    Myr. I know no evil death can show, which life
Has not already shown to those who live
Embodied longest. If there be indeed
A shore, where mind survives, 'twill be as mind,
All unincorporate: or if there flits
A shadow of this cumbrous clog of clay,
Which stalks, methinks, between our souls and
        heaven,
And fetters us to earth—at least the phantom,
Whate'er it have to fear, will not fear death.

    Sar. I fear it not; but I have felt—have seen—
A legion of the dead.

    Myr.   And so have I.
The dust we tread upon was once alive,
And wretched. But proceed: what hast thou seen?
Speak it, 'twill lighten thy dimm'd mind.

    Sar.   Methought——

Myr. Yet pause, thou art tired—in pain—ex-
        hausted; all
Which can impair both strength and spirit: seek
Rather to sleep again.

Sar.   Not now—I would not
Dream; though I know it now to be a dream
What I have dreamt:—and canst thou bear to hear it?

Myr. I can bear all things, dreams of life or death,
Which I participate with you, in semblance
Or full reality.

Sar.   And this look'd real,
I tell you: after that these eyes were open,
I saw them in their flight—for then they fled.

 Myr. Say on.

Sar.   I saw, that is, I dream'd myself
Here—here—even where we are, guests as we were,
Myself a host that deem'd himself but guest,
Willing to equal all in social freedom;
But, on my right hand and my left, instead
Of thee and Zames, and our custom'd meeting,
Was ranged on my left hand a haughty, dark,
And deadly face—I could not recognize it,
Yet I had seen it, though I knew not where;

The features were a giant's, and the eye
Was still, yet lighted; his long locks curl'd down
On his vast bust, whence a huge quiver rose
With shaft-heads feather'd from the eagle's wing,
That peep'd up bristling through his serpent hair.
I invited him to fill the cup which stood
Between us, but he answer'd not—I fill'd it—
He took it not, but stared upon me, till
I trembled at the fix'd glare of his eye:
I frown'd upon him as a king should frown—
He frown'd not in his turn, but look'd upon me
With the same aspect, which appall'd me more,
Because it changed not; and I turn'd for refuge
To milder guests, and sought them on the right,
Where thou wert wont to be.   But——

                              [*He pauses.*

 Myr.   What instead?
 Sar. In thy own chair—thy own place in the
   banquet—
I sought thy sweet face in the circle—but
Instead—a gray-hair'd, wither'd, bloody-eyed,
And bloody-handed, ghastly, ghostly thing,
Female in garb, and crown'd upon the brow,

Furrow'd with years, yet sneering with the passion
Of vengeance, leering too with that of lust,
Sate:—my veins curdled.

   Myr.   Is this all?

   Sar.   Upon
Her right hand—her lank, bird-like right hand—
      stood
A goblet, bubbling o'er with blood; and on
Her left, another, fill'd with—what I saw not,
But turn'd from it and her.   But all along
The table sate a range of crowned wretches,
Of various aspects, but of one expression.

   Myr. And felt you not this a mere vision?

   Sar.   No:
It was so palpable, I could have touch'd them.
I turn'd from one face to another, in
The hope to find at last one which I knew
Ere I saw theirs: but no—all turn'd upon me;
And stared, but neither ate nor drank, but stared,
Till I grew stone, as they seem'd half to be,
Yet breathing stone, for I felt life in them,
And life in me: there was a horrid kind
Of sympathy between us, as if they
Had lost a part of death to come to me,

And I the half of life to sit by them.
We were in an existence all apart
From heaven or earth——And rather let me see
Death all than such a being!

    Myr.   And the end?

    Sar. At last I sate marble, as they, when rose
The hunter, and the crew; and smiling on me—
Yes, the enlarged but noble aspect of
The hunter smiled upon me—I should say,
His lips, for his eyes moved not—and the woman's
Thin lips relax'd to something like a smile.
Both rose, and the crown'd figures on each hand
Rose also, as if aping their chief shades—
Mere mimics even in death—but I sate still:
A desperate courage crept through every limb,
And at the last I fear'd them not, but laugh'd
Full in their phantom faces. But then—then
The hunter laid his hand on mine: I took it,
And grasp'd it—but it melted from my own,
While he too vanish'd, and left nothing but
The memory of a hero, for he look'd so.

    Myr. And was: the ancestor of heroes, too,
And thine no less.

    Sar.   Ay, Myrrha, but the woman,

The female who remain'd, she flew upon me,
And burnt my lips up with her noisome kisses,
And, flinging down the goblets on each hand,
Methought their poisons flow'd around us, till
Each form'd a hideous river. Still she clung;
The other phantoms, like a row of statues,
Stood dull as in our temples, but she still
Embraced me, while I shrunk from her, as if,
In lieu of her remote descendant, I
Had been the son who slew her for her incest.
Then—then—a chaos of all loathsome things
Throng'd thick and shapeless: I was dead, yet
        feeling—
Buried, and raised again—consumed by worms,
Purged by the flames, and wither'd in the air!
I can fix nothing further of my thoughts,
Save that I long'd for thee, and sought for thee,
In all these agonies, and woke and found thee.

  Myr. So shalt thou find me ever at thy side,
Here and hereafter, if the last may be.
But think not of these things—the mere creations
Of late events acting upon a frame
Unused to toil, yet over-wrought by toil
Such as might try the sternest.

Sar.   I am better.
Now that I see thee once more, what was seen
Seems nothing.

Enter SALEMENES.

Sal.   Is the king so soon awake?
Sar. Yes, brother, and I would I had not slept;
For all the predecessors of our line
Rose up, methought, to drag me down to them.
My father was amongst them, too; but he,
I know not why, kept from me, leaving me
Between the hunter-founder of our race,
And her, the homicide and husband-killer,
Whom you call glorious.
Sal.   So I term you also,
Now you have shown a spirit like to hers.
By day-break I propose that we set forth,
And charge once more the rebel crew, who still
Keep gathering head, repulsed, but not quite quell'd.
Sar. How wears the night?
Sal.   There yet remain some hours
Of darkness: use them for your further rest.

Sar. No, not to-night, if 'tis not gone: me-
        thought
I pass'd hours in that vision.

Myr.   Scarcely one;
I watch'd by you: it was a heavy hour,
But an hour only.

Sar.   Let us then hold council;
To-morrow we set forth.

Sal.   But ere that time,
I had a grace to seek.

Sar.   'Tis granted.

Sal.   Hear it
Ere you reply too readily; and 'tis
For *your* ear only.

Myr.   Prince, I take my leave.

                    [*Exit* MYRRHA.

Sal. That slave deserves her freedom.

Sar.   Freedom only!
That slave deserves to share a throne.

Sal.   Your patience—
'Tis not yet vacant, and 'tis of its partner
I come to speak with you.

Sar.   How! of the queen?

Sal. Even so. I judged it fitting for their safety,

That, ere the dawn, she sets forth with her chil-
    dren
For Paphlagonia, where our kinsman Cotta
Governs; and there at all events secure
My nephews and your sons their lives, and with
    them
Their just pretensions to the crown in case——

    Sar. I perish—as is probable: well thought—
Let them set forth with a sure escort.

    Sal.   That
Is all provided, and the galley ready
To drop down the Euphrates; but ere they
Depart, will you not see——

    Sar.   My sons? It may
Unman my heart, and the poor boys will weep;
And what can I reply to comfort them,
Save with some hollow hopes, and ill-worn smiles?
You know I cannot feign.

    Sal.   But you can feel;
At least, I trust so: in a word, the queen
Requests to see you ere you part—for ever.

    Sar. Unto what end? what purpose? I will grant
Aught—all that she can ask—but such a meeting.

Sal. You know, or ought to know, enough of wo-
  men,
Since you have studied them so steadily,
That what they ask in aught that touches on
The heart, is dearer to their feelings or
Their fancy, than the whole external world.
I think as you do of my sister's wish;
But 'twas her wish—she is my sister—you
Her husband—will you grant it?
  Sar.   'Twill be useless:
But let her come.
  Sal. I go. [*Exit* SALEMENES.
  Sar.   We have lived asunder
Too long to meet again—and *now* to meet!
Have I not cares enow, and pangs enow,
To bear alone, that we must mingle sorrows,
Who have ceased to mingle love?

   Re-enter SALEMENES *and* ZARINA.

 Sal.   My sister! Courage:
Shame not our blood with trembling, but remember
From whence we sprung. The queen is present,
  sire.

Zar. I pray thee, brother, leave me.

Sal.   Since you ask it.

                              [*Exit* SALEMENES.

Zar. Alone with him! How many a year has past,
Though we are still so young, since we have met,
Which I have worn in widowhood of heart.
He loved me not: yet he seems little changed—
Changed to me only—would the change were mu-
          tual!
He speaks not—scarce regards me—not a word—
Nor look—yet he *was* soft of voice and aspect,
Indifferent, not austere.   My lord!

Sar.   Zarina!

Zar. No, *not* Zarina—do not say Zarina.
That tone—that word—annihilate long years,
And things which make them longer.

Sar.   'Tis too late
To think of these past dreams.   Let's not re-
          proach—
That is, reproach me not—for the *last* time——

Zar. And *first*.   I ne'er reproach'd you.

Sar.   'Tis most true;
And that reproof comes heavier on my heart
Than——But our hearts are not in our own power.

Zar. Nor hands; but I gave both.

Sar.   Your brother said,
It was your will to see me, ere you went
From Nineveh with—— (*He hesitates*).

Zar.   Our children: it is true.
I wish'd to thank you that you have not divided
My heart from all that's left it now to love—
Those who are yours and mine, who look like you,
And look upon me as you look'd upon me
Once——But they have not changed.

Sar.   Nor ever will.
I fain would have them dutiful.

Zar.   I cherish
Those infants, not alone from the blind love .
Of a fond mother, but as a fond woman.
They are now the only tie between us.

Sar. ·   Deem not
I have not done you justice: rather make them
Resemble your own line, than their own sire.
I trust them with you—to you: fit them for
A throne, or, if that be denied——You have heard
Of this night's tumults?

Zar.   I had half forgotten,

And could have welcomed any grief, save yours,
Which gave me to behold your face again.

    Ser. The throne—I say it not in fear—but 'tis
In peril; they perhaps may never mount it:
But let them not for this lose sight of it.
I will dare all things to bequeath it them;
But if I fail, then they must win it back
Bravely—and, won, wear it wisely, not as I
Have wasted down my royalty.

    Zar.   They ne'er
Shall know from me of aught but what may honour
Their father's memory.

    Sar.   Rather let them hear
The truth from you than from a trampling world.
If they be in adversity, they 'll learn
Too soon the scorn of crowds for crownless princes,
And find that all their father's sins are theirs.
My boys!—I could have borne it were I childless.

    Zar. Oh! do not say so—do not poison all
My peace left, by unwishing that thou wert
A father.   If thou conquerest, they shall reign,
And honour him who saved the realm for them,
So little cared for as his own; and if——

Sar. 'Tis lost, all earth will cry out thank your
    father!
And they will swell the echo with a curse.

    Zar. That they shall never do; but rather ho-
    nour
The name of him, who, dying like a king,
In his last hours did more for his own memory
Than many monarchs in a length of days,
Which date the flight of time, but make no annals.

    Sar. Our annals draw perchance unto their close;
But at the least, whate'er the past, their end
Shall be like their beginning—memorable.

    Zar. Yet, be not rash—be careful of your life,
Live but for those who love.

    Sar.   And who are they?
A slave, who loves from passion—I 'll not say
Ambition—she has seen thrones shake, and loves;
A few friends, who have revell'd till we are
As one, for they are nothing if I fall;
A brother I have injured—children whom
I have neglected, and a spouse——

    Zar.   Who loves

    Sar. And pardons?

Zar.   I have never thought of this,
And cannot pardon till I have condemn'd.

Sar. My wife!

Zar.   Now blessings on thee for that word!
I never thought to hear it more—from thee.

Sar. Oh! thou wilt hear it from my subjects.
          Yes—
These slaves, whom I have nurtured, pamper'd, fed,
And swoln with peace, and gorged with plenty, till
They reign themselves—all monarchs in their man-
          sions—
Now swarm forth in rebellion, and demand
His death, who made their lives a jubilee;
While the few upon whom I have no. claim
Are faithful! This is true, yet monstrous.

Zar.   'Tis
Perhaps too natural; for benefits
Turn poison in bad minds.

Sar.   And good ones make
Good out of evil. Happier than the bee,
Which hives not but from wholesome flowers.

Zar.   Then reap
The honey, nor inquire whence 'tis derived.
Be satisfied—you are not all abandon'd.

Sar. My life insures me that.   How long, bethink
    you,
Were not I yet a king, should I be mortal;
That is, where mortals *are*, not where they must
    be ?

Zar. I know not.   But yet live for my—that is,
Your children's sake!

Sar.   My gentle, wrong'd Zarina!
I am the very slave of circumstance
And impulse—borne away with every breath!
Misplaced upon the throne—misplaced in life.
I know not what I could have been, but feel
I am not what I should be—let it end.
But take this with thee: if I was not form'd
To prize a love like thine, a mind like thine,
Nor dote even on thy beauty—as I've doted
On lesser charms, for no cause save that such
Devotion was a duty, and I hated
All that look'd like a chain for me or others,
(This even rebellion must avouch); yet hear
These words, perhaps among my last—that none
Ere valued more thy virtues, though he knew not
To profit by them—as the miner lights

K

Upon a vein of virgin ore, discovering
That which avails him nothing : he hath found it,
But 'tis not his—but some superior's, who
Placed him to dig, but not divide the wealth
Which sparkles at his feet; nor dare he lift
Nor poise it, but must grovel on upturning
The sullen earth.

    Zar.   Oh ! if thou hast at length
Discover'd that my love is worth esteem,
I ask no more—but let us hence together,
And *I*—let me say *we*—shall yet be happy.
Assyria is not all the earth—we 'll find
A world out of our own—and be more blest
Than I have ever been, or thou, with all
An empire to indulge thee.

Enter SALEMENES.

    Sal.   I must part ye—
The moments, which must not be lost, are passing.

    Zar. Inhuman brother! wilt thou thus weigh out
Instants so high and blest?

    Sal.   Blest!

Zar. He hath been
So gentle with me, that I cannot think
Of quitting.

Sal. So—this feminine farewell
Ends as such partings end, in *no* departure.
I thought as much, and yielded against all
My better bodings. But it must not be.

Zar. Not be?

Sal. Remain, and perish——

Zar. With my husband——

Sal. And children.

Zar. Alas!

Sal. Hear me, sister, like
My sister:—all 's prepared to make your safety
Certain, and of the boys too, our last hopes
'Tis not a single question of mere feeling,
Though that were much—but 'tis a point of state:
The rebels would do more to seize upon
The offspring of their sovereign, and so crush——

Zar. Ah! do not name it.

Sal. Well, then, mark me: when
They are safe beyond the Median's grasp, the rebels
Have miss'd their chief aim—the extinction of

The line of Nimrod. Though the present king
Fall, his sons live for victory and vengeance.

Zar. But could not I remain, alone?

Sal.   What! leave
Your children, with two parents and yet orphans—
In a strange land—so young, so distant?

Zar.   No—
My heart will break.

Sal.   Now you know all—decide.

Sar. Zarina, he hath spoken well, and we
Must yield awhile to this necessity.
Remaining here, you may lose all; departing,
You save the better part of what is left
To both of us, and to such loyal hearts
As yet beat in these kingdoms.

Sal.   The time presses.

Sar. Go, then. If e'er we meet again, perhaps
I may be worthier of you—and, if not,
Remember that my faults, though not atoned for,
Are *ended.*   Yet, I dread thy nature will
Grieve more above the blighted name and ashes
Which once were mightiest in Assyria—than——
But I grow womanish again, and must not;

I must learn sternness now.   My sins have all
Been of the softer order——*hide* thy tears—
I do not bid thee *not* to shed them—'t were
Easier to stop Euphrates at its source
Than one tear of a true and tender heart—
But let me not behold them; they unman me
Here when I had remann'd myself.   My brother,
Lead her away.

    Zar.   Oh, God! I never shall
Behold him more!

    Sal. (*striving to conduct her*).   Nay, sister, I *must*
        be obey'd.

    Zar. I must remain—away! you shall not hold
        me.
What, shall he die alone?—*I* live alone?

    Sal. He shall *not die alone;* but lonely you
Have lived for years.

    Zar.   That's false! I knew *he* lived,
And lived upon his image—let me go!

    Sal. (*conducting her off the stage*). Nay, then, I
        must use some fraternal force,
Which you will pardon.

    Zar.   Never.   Help me! Oh!

Sardanapalus, wilt thou thus behold me
Torn from thee?

 Sal.   Nay—then all is lost again,
If that this moment is not gain'd.

 Zar.   My brain turns—
My eyes fail—where is he?   [*She faints.*

 Sar. (advancing).   No—set her down—
She 's dead—and you have slain her.

 Sal. .   'Tis the mere
Faintness of o'er-wrought passion: in the air
She will recover. Pray, keep back.—[*Aside.*] I
   must
Avail myself of this sole moment to
Bear her to where her children are embark'd,
I' the royal galley on the river.

      [SALEMENES *bears her off.*

 Sar. (solus).   This, too—
And this too must I suffer—I, who never
Inflicted purposely on human hearts
A voluntary pang! But that is false—
She loved me, and I loved her. Fatal passion!
Why dost thou not expire *at once* in hearts
Which thou hast lighted up at once? Zarina!

I must pay dearly for the desolation
Now brought upon thee.   Had I never loved
But thee, I should have been an unopposed
Monarch of honouring nations.   To what gulfs
A single deviation from the track
Of human duties leads even those who claim
The homage of mankind as their born due,
And find it, till they forfeit it themselves!

Enter MYRRHA.

   Sar. *You* here!   Who call'd you?
   Myr.   No one—but I heard
Far off a voice of wail and lamentation,
And thought——
   Sar.   It forms no portion of your duties
To enter here till sought for.
   Myr.   Though I might,
Perhaps, recal some softer words of yours
(Although they *too were chiding*), which reproved
     me,
Because I ever dreaded to intrude;
Resisting my own wish and your injunction

To heed no time nor presence, but approach you
Uncall'd for: I retire.

Sal.   Yet stay—being here.
I pray you pardon me: events have sour'd me
Till I wax peevish—heed it not: I shall
Soon be myself again.

Myr.   I wait with patience,
What I shall see with pleasure.

Sar.   Scarce a moment
Before your entrance in this hall, Zarina,
Queen of Assyria, departed hence.

Myr. Ah!

Sar.   Wherefore do you start?

Myr.   Did I do so?

Sar. 'Twas well you entered by another portal,
Else you had met. That pang at least is spared
        her!

Myr. I know to feel for her.

Sar.   That is too much,
And beyond nature—'tis nor mutual
Nor possible. You cannot pity her,
Nor she aught but——

Myr.   Despise the favourite slave?
Not more than I have ever scorn'd myself.

Sar. Scorn'd! what, to be the envy of your sex,
And lord it o'er the heart of the world's lord?

    Myr. Were you the lord of twice ten thousand
        worlds—
As you are like to lose the one you sway'd—
I did abase myself as much in being
Your paramour, as though you were a peasant—
Nay, more, if that the peasant were a Greek.

    Sar. You talk it well——

    Myr.   And truly.

    Sar.   In the hour
Of man's adversity all things grow daring
Against the falling; but as I am not
Quite fall'n, nor now disposed to bear reproaches,
Perhaps because I merit them too often,
Let us then part while peace is still between us.

    Myr. Part!

    Sar.   Have not all past human beings parted,
And must not all the present one day part?

    Myr. Why?

    Sar. For your safety, which I will have look'd
        to,
With a strong escort to your native land;

And such gifts, as, if you have not been all
A queen, shall make your dowry worth a kingdom.

    Myr. I pray you talk not thus.

    Sar.   The queen is gone:
You need not shame to follow. I would fall
Alone—I seek no partners but in pleasure.

    Myr. And I no pleasure but in parting not.
You shall not force me from you.

    Sar.   Think well of it—
It soon may be too late.

    Myr.   So let it be;
For then you cannot separate me from you.

    Sar. And will not; but I thought you wish'd it.

    Myr.   I !

    Sar. You spoke of your abasement.

    Myr.   And I feel it
Deeply—more deeply than all things but love.

    Sar. Then fly from it.

    Myr.   'Twill not recal the past—
'Twill not restore my honour, nor my heart.
No—here I stand or fall. If that you conquer,
I live to joy in your great triumph; should
Your lot be different, I 'll not weep, but share it.
You did not doubt me a few hours ago.

Sar. Your courage never—nor your love till now;
And none could make me doubt it save yourself.
Those words——

    Myr.   Were words. I pray you, let the proofs
Be in the past acts you were pleased to praise
This very night, and in my further bearing,
Beside, wherever you are borne by fate.

    Sar. I am content: and, trusting in my cause,
Think we may yet be victors and return
To peace—the only victory I covet.
To me war is no glory—conquest no
Renown. To be forced thus to uphold my right
Sits heavier on my heart than all the wrongs
These men would bow me down with. Never,
         never
Can I forget this night, even should I live
To add it to the memory of others.
I thought to have made mine inoffensive rule
An era of sweet peace 'midst bloody annals,
A green spot amidst desert centuries,
On which the future would turn back and smile,
And cultivate, or sigh when it could not
Recal Sardanapalus' golden reign.

I thought to have made my realm a paradise,
And every moon an epoch of new pleasures.
I took the rabble's shouts for love—the breath
Of friends for truth—the lips of woman for
My only guerdon—so they are, my Myrrha:

                    [*He kisses her.*

Kiss me. Now let them take my realm and life!
They shall have both, but never thee!
   Myr.   No, never!
Man may despoil his brother man of all
That's great or glittering—kingdoms fall—hosts
       yield—
Friends fail—slaves fly—and all betray—and, more
Than all, the most indebted—but a heart
That loves without self-love! 'Tis here—now prove
       it.

             Enter SALEMENES.

   Sal. I sought you.—How! *she* here again?
   Sar.   Return not
Now to reproof: methinks your aspect speaks
Of higher matter than a woman's presence.

Sal. The only woman whom it much imports
  me
At such a moment now is safe in absence—
The queen 's embark'd.
 Sar.   And well? say that much.
 Sal.   Yes.
Her transient weakness has pass'd o'er; at least,
It settled into tearless silence: her
Pale face and glittering eye, after a glance
Upon her sleeping children, were still fix'd
Upon the palace towers as the swift galley
Stole down the hurrying stream beneath the star-
  light;
But she said nothing.
 Sar.   Would I felt no more
Than she has said!
 Sal.   'Tis now too late to feel!
Your feelings cannot cancel a sole pang;
To change them, my advices bring sure tidings
That the rebellious Medes and Chaldees, mar-
  shall'd
By their two leaders, are already up
In arms again; and, serrying their ranks,

Prepare to attack: they have apparently
Been join'd by other satraps.

    Sar.   What! more rebels?
Let us be first, then.

    Sal.   That were hardly prudent
Now, though it was our first intention.   If
By noon to-morrow we are join'd by those
I've sent for by sure messengers, we shall be
In strength enough to venture an attack,
Ay, and pursuit too; but till then, my voice
Is to await the onset.

    Sar.   I detest
That waiting; though it seems so safe to fight
Behind high walls, and hurl down foes into
Deep fosses, or behold them sprawl on spikes
Strew'd to receive them, still I like it not—
My soul seems lukewarm; but when I set on them,
Though they were piled on mountains, I would
            have
A pluck at them, or perish in hot blood!—
Let me then charge!

    Sal.   You talk like a young soldier.

    Sar. I am no soldier, but a man: speak not

Of soldiership, I loathe the word, and those
Who pride themselves upon it; but direct me
Where I may pour upon them.

    Sal.   You must spare
To expose your life too hastily; 'tis not
Like mine or any other subject's breath:
The whole war turns upon it—with it; this
Alone creates it, kindles, and may quench it—
Prolong it—end it.

    Sar.   Then let us end both!
'Twere better thus, perhaps, than prolong either;
I 'm sick of one, perchance of both.

                       [*A trumpet sounds without.*

    Sal.   · Hark!

    Sar.   Let us
Reply, not listen.

    Sal.   And your wound!

    Sar.   'Tis bound—
'Tis heal'd—I had forgotten it.   Away!
A leech's lancet would have scratch'd me deeper;
The slave that gave it might be well ashamed
To have struck so weakly.

    Sal.   Now, may none this hour
Strike with a better aim!

†

Sar.   Ay, if we conquer;
But if not, they will only leave to me
A task they might have spared their king.   Upon
          them!   [*Trumpet sounds again.*
  Sal. I am with you.
    Sar.   Ho, my arms! again, my arms!
                                        [*Exeunt.*

ACT V. SCENE I.

The same Hall of the Palace.

MYRRHA *and* BALEA.

Myr. (*at a window*). The day at last has broken.
        What a night
Hath usher'd it! How beautiful in heaven!
Though varied with a transitory storm,
More beautiful in that variety!
How hideous upon earth! where peace and hope,
And love and revel, in an hour were trampled
By human passions to a human chaos,
Not yet resolved to separate elements.—
'Tis warring still! And can the sun so rise,
So bright, so rolling back the clouds into
Vapours more lovely than the unclouded sky
With golden pinnacles, and snowy mountains,
And billows purpler than the ocean's, making
In heaven a glorious mockery of the earth,
So like we almost deem it permanent;

So fleeting, we can scarcely call it aught
Beyond a vision, 'tis so transiently
Scatter'd along the eternal vault : and yet
It dwells upon the soul, and soothes the soul,
And blends itself into the soul, until
Sunrise and sunset form the haunted epoch
Of sorrow and of love ; which they who mark not,
Know not the realms where those twin genii
(Who chasten and who purify our hearts,
So that we would not change their sweet rebukes
For all the boisterous joys that ever shook
The air with clamour), build the palaces
Where their fond votaries repose and breathe
Briefly ;—but in that brief cool calm inhale
Enough of heaven to enable them to bear
The rest of common, heavy, human hours,
And dream them through in placid sufferance ;
Though seemingly employ'd like all the rest
Of toiling breathers in allotted tasks
Of pain or pleasure, *two* names for *one* feeling,
Which our internal, restless agony
Would vary in the sound, although the sense
Escapes our highest efforts to be happy.

 Bal. You muse right calmly: and can you so
   watch
The sunrise which may be our last?

 Myr.   It is
Therefore that I so watch it, and reproach
Those eyes, which never may behold it more,
For having look'd upon it oft, too oft,
Without the reverence and the rapture due
To that which keeps all earth from being as fragile
As I am in this form.   Come, look upon it,
The Chaldee's god, which, when I gaze upon,
I grow almost a convert to your Baal.

 Bal. As now he reigns in heaven, so once on
   earth
He sway'd.

 Myr.   He sways it now far more, then; never
Had earthly monarch half the peace and glory
Which centres in a single ray of his.

 Bal. Surely he is a god!

 Myr.   So we Greeks deem too;
And yet I sometimes think that gorgeous orb
Must rather be the abode of gods than one
Of the immortal sovereigns.   Now he breaks

            L 2

Through all the clouds, and fills my eyes with light
That shuts the world out.   I can look no more.

 Bal. Hark! heard you not a sound?

 Myr.   No, 'twas mere fancy;
They battle it beyond the wall, and not
As in late midnight conflict in the very
Chambers: the palace has become a fortress
Since that insidious hour; and here within
The very centre, girded by vast courts
And regal halls of pyramid proportions,
Which must be carried one by one before
They penetrate to where they then arrived,
We are as much shut in even from the sound
Of peril as from glory.

 Bal.   But they reach'd
Thus far before.

 Myr.   Yes, by surprise, and were
Beat back by valour; now at once we have
Courage and vigilance to guard us.

 Bal.   May they
Prosper!

 Myr. That is the prayer of many, and
The dread of more: it is an anxious hour;

I strive to keep it from my thoughts.   Alas!
How vainly!

   Bal.   It is said the king's demeanour
In the late action scarcely more appall'd
The rebels than astonish'd his true subjects.

   Myr. 'Tis easy to astonish or appal
The vulgar mass which moulds a horde of slaves;
But he did bravely.

   Bal.   Slew he not Beleses?
I heard the soldiers say he struck him down.

   Myr. The wretch was overthrown, but rescued to
Triumph, perhaps, o'er one who vanquish'd him
In fight, as he had spared him in his peril;
And by that heedless pity risk'd a crown.

   Bal. Hark!

   Myr. You are right; some steps approach, but
      slowly.

Enter Soldiers, bearing in SALEMENES *wounded,
with a broken Javelin in his Side: they seat him
upon one of the Couches which furnish the Apartment.*

Myr. Oh, Jove!

Bal.   Then all is over.

Sal.   That is false.
Hew down the slave who says so, if a soldier.

Myr. Spare him—he's none: a mere court but-
        terfly,
That flutters in the pageant of a monarch.

Sal. Let him live on, then.

Myr.   So wilt thou, I trust.

Sal. I fain would live this hour out, and the
        event,
But doubt it. Wherefore did ye bear me here?

Sol. By the king's order. When the javelin struck
        you,
You fell and fainted; 'twas his strict command
To bear you to this hall.

Sal.   'Twas not ill done:

For seeming slain in that cold dizzy trance,
The sight might shake our soldiers—but—'tis vain,
I feel it ebbing!

 Myr.   Let me see the wound ;
I am not quite skilless : in my native land
'Tis part of our instruction. War being constant,
We are nerved to look on such things.

 Sol.   Best extract
The javelin.

 Myr. Hold ! no, no, it cannot be.

 Sal. I am sped, then !

 Myr. With the blood that fast must follow
The extracted weapon, I do fear thy life.

 Sal. And I *not* death. Where was the king when
   you
Convey'd me from the spot where I was stricken?

 Sol. Upon the same ground, and encouraging
With voice and gesture the dispirited troops .
Who had seen you fall, and falter'd back.

 Sal.   Whom heard ye
Named next to the command?

 Sol.   . I did not hear.

 Sal. Fly, then, and tell him, 'twas my last request

That Zames take my post until the junction,
So hoped for, yet delay'd, of Ofratanes,
Satrap of Susa. Leave me here: our troops
Are not so numerous as to spare your absence.

  Sol. But, prince——

  Sal.   Hence, I say! Here's a courtier and
A woman, the best chamber company.
As you would not permit me to expire
Upon the field, I'll have no idle soldiers
About my sick couch. Hence! and do my bidding!

        [*Exeunt the Soldiers.*

  Myr. Gallant and glorious spirit! must the earth
So soon resign thee?

  Sal.   Gentle Myrrha, 'tis
The end I would have chosen, had I saved
The monarch or the monarchy by this;
As 'tis, I have not outlived them.

  Myr.   You wax paler.

  Sal. Your hand; this broken weapon but prolongs
My pangs, without sustaining life enough
To make me useful: I would draw it forth
And my life with it, could I but hear how
The fight goes.

Enter SARDANAPALUS *and Soldiers.*

Sar.   My best brother!

Sal.   And the battle
Is lost?

Sar. (*despondingly*). You see *me here.*

Sal.   I 'd rather see you *thus !*
          [*He draws out the weapon from the wound,*
              and dies.

Sar. And *thus* I will be seen; unless the suc-
          cour,   .
The last frail reed of our beleaguer'd hopes,
Arrive with Ofratanes.

Myr.   .   Did you not
Receive a token from your dying brother,
Appointing Zames chief?

Sar.   I did.

Myr.   Where 's Zames?

Sar. Dead.

Myr.   And Altada?

Sar.   Dying.

Myr.   Pania? Sfero? .

Sar. Pania yet lives; but Sfero 's fled, or captive.
I am alone.

Myr.   And is all lost?

Sar.   Our walls,
Though thinly mann'd, may still hold out against
Their present force, or aught save treachery:
But i' the field——

    Myr.   I thought 'twas the intent
Of Salemenes not to risk a sally
Till ye were strengthen'd by the expected succours.

    Sar. I overruled him.

    Myr.   Well, the fault 's a brave one.

    Sar. But fatal. Oh, my brother! I would give
These realms, of which thou wert the ornament,
The sword and shield, the sole-redeeming honour,
To call back——But I will not weep for thee;
Thou shalt be mourn'd for as thou wouldst be
          mourn'd.
It grieves me most that thou couldst quit this life
Believing that I could survive what thou
Hast died for—our long royalty of race.
If I redeem it, I will give thee blood
Of thousands, tears of millions, for atonement,
(The tears of all the good are thine already.)
If not, we meet again soon, if the spirit
Within us lives beyond:—thou readest mine,

And dost me justice now.   Let me once clasp
That yet warm hand, and fold that throbless heart
[Embraces the body.
To this which beats so bitterly.   Now, bear
The body hence.

    Soldier.   Where?

    Sar.   To my proper chamber.
Place it beneath my canopy, as though
The king lay there: when this is done, we will
Speak further of the rites due to such ashes.

    [*Exeunt Soldiers with the body of* SALEMENES.

Enter PANIA.

    Sar. Well, Pania! have you placed the guards,
        and issued
The orders fix'd on?

    Pan.   Sire, I have obey'd.

    Sar. And do the soldiers keep their hearts up?

    Pan.   Sire?

    Sar. I'm answer'd!   When a king asks twice,
        and has

A question as an answer to *his* question,
It is a portent.   What! they are dishearten'd?
  Pan. The death of Salemenes, and the shouts
Of the exulting rebels on his fall,
Have made them——
  Sar.   *Rage*—not droop—it should have been.
We'll find the means to rouse them.
  Pan.   Such a loss
Might sadden even a victory.
  Sar.   Alas!
Who can so feel it as I feel? but yet,
Though coop'd within these walls, they are strong,
          and we
Have those without will break their way through
          hosts,
To make their sovereign's dwelling what it was—
A palace; not a prison, nor a fortress.

               Enter an Officer, hastily.

  Sar. Thy face seems ominous.   Speak!
  Off.   I dare not.

Sar.   Dare not?
While millions dare revolt with sword in hand!
That's strange. I pray thee break that loyal silence
Which loathes to shock its sovereign ; we can hear
Worse than thou hast to tell.

  Pan.   Proceed, thou hearest.

  Offi. The wall which skirted near the river's brink
Is thrown down by the sudden inundation
Of the Euphrates, which now rolling, swoln
From the enormous mountains where it rises,
By the late rains of that tempestuous region,
O'erfloods its banks, and hath destroy'd the bul-
          wark.

  Pan. That's a black augury! it has been said
For ages, " That the city ne'er should yield
" To man, until the river grew its foe."

  Sar. I can forgive the omen, not the ravage.
How much is swept down of the wall?

  Offi.   About
Some twenty stadii.

  Sar.   And all this is left
Pervious to the assailants?

  Offi.   For the present

The river's fury must impede the assault;
But when he shrinks into his wonted channel,
And may be cross'd by the accustom'd barks,
The palace is their own.

  Sar.   That shall be never.
Though men, and gods, and elements, and omens,
Have risen up 'gainst one who ne'er provoked them,
My fathers' house shall never be a cave
For wolves to horde and howl in.

  Pan.   With your sanction
I will proceed to the spot, and take such measures
For the assurance of the vacant space
As time and means permit.

  Sar.   About it straight,
And bring me back as speedily as full
And fair investigation may permit
Report of the true state of this irruption
Of waters.   [*Exeunt* PANIA *and the Officer.*

  Myr. Thus the very waves rise up
Against you.

  Sar. They are not my subjects, girl,
And may be pardon'd, since they can't be punish'd.

  Myr. I joy to see this portent shakes you not.

Sar. I am past the fear of portents : they can tell
      me
Nothing I have not told myself since midnight :
Despair anticipates such things.

  Myr.   Despair !

  Sar. No ; not despair precisely. When we know
All that can come, and how to meet it, our
Resolves, if firm, may merit a more noble
Word than this is to give it utterance.
But what are words to us ? we have well nigh done
With them and all things.

  Myr.   Save *one deed*—the last
And greatest to all mortals ; crowning act
Of all that was—or is—or is to be—   .
The only thing common to all mankind,
So different in their births, tongues, sexes, natures,
Hues, features, climes, times, feelings, intellects,
· Without one point of union save in this,
To which we tend, for which we 're born, and
      thread
The labyrinth of mystery, call'd life.

  Sar. Our clew being well nigh wound out, let 's be
      cheerful.

They who have nothing more to fear may well
Indulge a smile at that which once appall'd;
As children at discover'd bugbears.

Re-enter PANIA.

   Pan.   'Tis
As was reported: I have order'd there
A double guard, withdrawing from the wall
Where it was strongest the required addition
To watch the breach occasion'd by the waters.
   Sar. You have done your duty faithfully, and as
My worthy Pania! further ties between us
Draw near a close. I pray you take this key:
                       [*Gives a key.*
It opens to a secret chamber, placed
Behind the couch in my own chamber. (Now
Press'd by a nobler weight than e'er it bore—
Though a long line of sovereigns have lain down
Along its golden frame—as bearing for
A time what late was Salemenes). Search
The secret covert to which this will lead you;

'Tis full of treasure; take it for yourself
And your companions: there's.enough to load ye,
Though ye be many.   Let the slaves be freed, too;
And all the inmates of the palace, of
Whatever sex, now quit it in an hour.
Thence launch the regal barks, once form'd for plea-
        sure,
And now to serve for safety, and embark.
The river's broad and swoln, and uncommanded
(More potent than a king) by these besiegers.
Fly! and be happy!
    Pan.   Under your protection!
So you accompany your faithful guard.
    Sar.   No, Pania! that must not be; get thee
        hence,
And leave me to my fate.
    Pan.   'Tis the first time
I ever disobey'd: but now ——
    Sar.   So all men
Dare beard me now, and Insolence within
Apes Treason from without.   Question no further;
'Tis my command, my last command.   Wilt *thou*
Oppose it? *thou!*

                                M

Pan.   But yet—not yet.

Sar.   ·   ·   Well, then,
Swear that you will obey when I shall give
The signal.

Pan.   With a heavy but true heart,
I promise.

Sar.   'Tis enough.   Now order here
Faggots, pine-nuts, and wither'd leaves, and such
Things as catch fire and blaze with one sole spark ;
Bring cedar, too, and precious drugs, and spices,
And mighty planks, to nourish a tall pile ;
Bring frankincense and myrrh, too, for it is
For a great sacrifice I build the pyre ;
And heap them round yon throne.

Pan.   My lord!

Sar.   I have said it,
And *you* have *sworn.*

Pan.   And could keep my faith
Without a vow.   [*Exit* PANIA.

Myr.   What mean you?

Sar.   You shall know
Anon—what the whole earth shall ne'er forget.

PANIA, *returning with a Herald.*

Pan. My king, in going forth upon my duty,
This herald has been brought before me, craving
An audience.
    Sal.   Let him speak.
    Her.   The *King* Arbaces——
    Sar. What, crown'd already?—But, proceed.
    Her.   Beleses,
The anointed high-priest ——
    Sar.   Of what god or demon?
With new kings rise new altars.   But, proceed;
You are sent to prate your master's will, and not
Reply to mine.
    Her.   And Satrap Ofratanes——
    Sar. Why, *he* is *ours.*
    Her. (*Showing a ring*). Be sure that he is now
In the camp of the conquerors ; behold
His signet ring.
    Sar.   'Tis his.   A worthy triad !
Poor Salemenes ! thou hast died in time
To see one treachery the less : this man

M 2

Was thy true friend and my most trusted subject.
Proceed.

    Her.   They offer thee thy life, and freedom
Of choice to single out a residence
In any of the further provinces,
Guarded and watch'd, but not confined in person,
Where thou shalt pass thy days in peace ; but on
Condition that the three young princes are
Given up as hostages.

    Sar. (*ironically*).   The generous victors !

    Her. I wait the answer.

    Sar.   Answer, slave ! How long
Have slaves decided on the doom of kings ?

    Her. Since they were free.

    Sar.   Mouthpiece of mutiny !
Thou at the least shalt learn the penalty
Of treason, though its proxy only.   Pania !
Let his head be thrown from our walls within
The rebels' lines, his carcass down the river.
Away with him !

                [PANIA *and the Guards seizing him.*

    Pan.   I never yet obey'd
Your orders with more pleasure than the present.
Hence with him, soldiers ! do not soil this hall

Of royalty with treasonable gore ;
Put him to rest without.

   Her.   A single word :
My office, king, is sacred.

   Sar.   And what's *mine ?*
That thou shouldst come and dare to ask of me
To lay it down ?

   Her.   I but obey'd my orders,
At the same peril if refused, as now
Incurr'd by my obedience.

   Sar.   So there are
New monarchs of an hour's growth as despotic
As sovereigns swathed in purple, and enthroned
From birth to manhood !

   Her.   My life waits your breath.
Yours (I speak humbly)—but it may be—yours
May also be in danger scarce less imminent :
Would it then suit the last hours of a line
Such as is that of Nimrod, to destroy
A peaceful herald, unarm'd, in his office ;
And violate not only all that man
Holds sacred between man and man—but that
More holy tie which links us with the gods ?

   Sar. He's right.—Let him go free.—My life's last act

Shall not be one of wrath.   Here, fellow, take
          [*Gives him a golden cup from a table near.*
This golden goblet, let it hold your wine,
And think of *me;* or melt it into ingots,
And think of nothing but their weight and value.

    Her. I thank you doubly for my life, and this
Most gorgeous gift, which renders it more precious.
But must I bear no answer?

    Sar.   Yes,—I ask
An hour's truce to consider.

    Her.   . But an hour's?

    Sar. An hour's: if at the expiration of
That time your masters hear no further from me,
They are to deem that I reject their terms,
And act befittingly.

    Her.   I shall not fail
To be a faithful legate of your pleasure.

    Sar. And, hark! a word more.

    Her.   I shall not forget it,
Whate'er it be.

    Sar.   Commend me to Beleses;
And tell him, ere a year expire, I summon
Him hence to meet me.

    Her.   Where?

Sar.   At Babylon.
At least from thence he will depart to meet me.
   Her. I shall obey you to the letter.
                              [*Exit Herald.*
   Sar.   Pania!—
Now, my good Pania!—quick—with what I order'd.
   Pan. My lord,—the soldiers are already charged.
And, see! they enter.
                  ]*Soldiers enter, and form a Pile about*
                    the Throne, &c.
   Sar.   Higher, my good soldiers,
And thicker yet; and see that the foundation
Be such as will not speedily exhaust
Its own too subtle flame; nor yet be quench'd
With aught officious aid would bring to quell it.
Let the throne form the *core* of it; I would not
Leave that, save fraught with fire unquenchable,
To the new comers. Frame the whole as if
'Twere to enkindle the strong tower of our
Inveterate enemies.   Now it bears an aspect!
How say you, Pania, will this pile suffice
For a king's obsequies?
   Pan.   Ay, for a kingdom's.
I understand you, now.

Sar.   And blame me?

Pan   No—

Let me but fire the pile, and share it with you.

   Myr. That duty's mine.

   Pan.   A woman's!

   Myr.   'Tis the soldier's

Part to die *for* his sovereign, and why not

The woman's with her lover?

   Pan.   'Tis most strange!

   Myr. But not so rare, my Pania, as thou think'st

      it.

In the mean time, live thou.—Farewell! the pile

Is ready.

   Pan. I should shame to leave my sovereign

With but a single female to partake

His death.

   Sar. Too many far have heralded

Me to the dust, already. Get thee hence;

Enrich thee.

   Pan. And live wretched!

   Sar.   Think upon

Thy vow;—'tis sacred and irrevocable.

   Pan. Since it is so, farewell.

   Sar.   Search well my chamber,

Feel no remorse at bearing off the gold ;
Remember, what you leave you leave the slaves
Who slew me: and when you have borne away
All safe off to your boats, blow one long blast
Upon the trumpet as you quit the palace.
The river's brink is too remote, its stream
Too loud at present to permit the echo
To reach distinctly from its banks.   Then fly,—
And as you sail, turn back ; but still keep on
Your way along the Euphrates: if you reach
The land of Paphlagonia, where the queen
Is safe with my three sons in Cotta's court,
Say what you *saw* at parting, and request
That she remember what I *said* at one
Parting more mournful still.
    Pan.   That royal hand !
Let me then once more press it to my lips ;
And these poor soldiers who throng round you, and
Would fain die with you !
       [*The Soldiers and* PANIA *throng round him,*
          kissing his hand and the hem of his robe.
.   *Sar.*   My best ! my last friends !
Let 's not unman each other—part at once :

All farewells should be sudden, when for ever,
Else they make an eternity of moments,
And clog the last sad sands of life with tears.
Hence, and be happy: trust me, I am not
Now to be pitied; or far more for what
Is past than present;—for the future, 'tis
In the hands of the deities, if such
There be: I shall know soon. Farewell—farewell.

                [*Exeunt* PANIA *and Soldiers.*

   Myr. These men were honest: it is comfort still
That our last looks should be on loving faces.

   Sar. And *lovely* ones, my beautiful!—but hear
      me!
If at this moment, for we now are on
The brink, thou feel'st an inward shrinking from
This leap through flame into the future, say it:
I shall not love thee less; nay, perhaps more,
For yielding to thy nature: and there's time
Yet for thee to escape hence.

   Myr.   Shall I light
One of the torches which lie heap'd beneath
The ever-burning lamp that burns without,
Before Baal's shrine, in the adjoining hall?

Sar. Do so. Is that thy answer?

Myr.   Thou shalt see.

                            [*Exit* MYRRHA.

Sar. (*solus.*) She's firm. My fathers! whom I
      will rejoin,
It may be, purified by death from some
Of the gross stains of too material being,
I would not leave your ancient first abode
To the defilement of usurping bondmen;
If I have not kept your inheritance
As ye bequeath'd it, this bright part of it,
Your treasure, your abode, your sacred relics
Of arms, and records, monuments, and spoils,
In which *they* would have revell'd, I bear with me
To you in that absorbing element,
Which most personifies the soul as leaving
The least of matter unconsumed before
Its fiery workings:—and the light of this
Most royal of funereal pyres shall be
Not a mere pillar form'd of cloud and flame,
A beacon in the horizon for a day,
And then a mount of ashes, but a light
To lesson ages, rebel nations, and
Voluptuous princes. Time shall quench full many

A people's records, and a hero's acts;
Sweep empire after empire, like this first
Of empires, into nothing; · but even then
Shall spare this deed of mine, and hold it up
A problem few dare imitate, and none
Despise—but, it may be, avoid the life
Which led to such a consummation.

MYRRHA *returns with a lighted Torch in her Hand,*
             and a Cup in the other.

Myr.   Lo!
I 've lit the lamp which lights us to the stars.
    Sar. And the cup?
    Myr.   'Tis my country's custom to
Make a libation to the gods.
    Sar.   And mine
To make libations amongst men. I 've not
Forgot the custom; and although alone,
Will drain one draught in memory of many
A joyous banquet past.
    [SARDANAPALUS *takes the cup, and after drinking*
       and tinkling the reversed cup, as a drop falls,
       exclaims—
                   And this libation
Is for the excellent Beleses.

Myr.　　　　　　　　Why
Dwells thy mind rather upon that man's name
Than on his mate's in villany?

Sar.　　　　　　　　The other
Is a mere soldier, a mere tool, a kind
Of human sword in a friend's hand; the other
Is master-mover of his warlike puppet:
But I dismiss them from my mind.—Yet pause,
My Myrrha! dost thou truly follow me,
Freely and fearlessly?

Myr.　　　　　　　And dost thou think
A Greek girl dare not do for love, that which
An Indian widow braves for custom?

Sar.　　　　　　　　Then
We but await the signal.

Myr.　　　　　　　It is long
In sounding.

Sar.　　Now, farewell; one last embrace.

Myr. Embrace, but *not* the last; there is one
　　　more.

Sar. True, the commingling fire will mix our
　　ashes.

Myr. And pure as is my love to thee, shall they,

Purged from the dross of earth, and earthly passion,
Mix pale with thine.   A single thought yet irks me.
  Sar. Say it.
  Myr.   It is that no kind hand will gather
The dust of both into one urn.
  Sar.   The better:
Rather let them be borne abroad upon
The winds of heaven, and scatter'd into air,
Than be polluted more by human hands
Of slaves and traitors; in this blazing palace,
And its enormous walls of reeking ruin,
We leave a nobler monument than Egypt
Hath piled in her brick mountains, o'er dead kings,
Or *kine,* for none know whether those proud piles
Be for their monarch, or their ox-god Apis:
So much for monuments that have forgotten
Their very record!
  Myr.   Then farewell, thou earth!
And loveliest spot of earth! farewell, Ionia!
Be thou still free and beautiful, and far
Aloof from desolation!   My last prayer
Was for thee, my last thoughts, save *one,* were of
        thee!

Sar. And that?

Myr.   Is yours.

          [*The trumpet of* PANIA *sounds without.*

Sar.   Hark!

Myr.   Now!

Sar.   Adieu, Assyria!

I loved thee well, my own, my fathers' land,
And better as my country than my kingdom.
I satiated thee with peace and joys; and this
Is my reward! and now I owe thee nothing,
Not even a grave.   [*He mounts the pile.*

          Now, Myrrha!

Myr.   Art thou ready?

Sar. As the torch in thy grasp.

          [MYRRHA *fires the pile.*

Myr.   'Tis fired! I come.

          [*As* MYRRHA *springs forward to throw herself
          into the flames, the Curtain falls.*

NOTES.

Note 1, page 8, lines 3 from bottom.

And thou, my own Ionian Myrrha.

" The Ionian name had been still more comprehensive, having
included the Achaians and the Bœotians, who, together with those
to whom it was afterwards confined, would make nearly the whole
of the Greek nation, and among the orientals it was always the
general name for the Greeks."—*Mitford's Greece*, vol. i. p. 199.

Note 2, page 22, lines 6 to 9.

————— " *Sardanapalus*
" *The king, and son of Anacyndaraxes,*
" *In one day built Anchialus and Tarsus.*
" *Eat, drink, and love; the rest's not worth a fillip.*"

" For this expedition he took only a small chosen body of
the phalanx, but all his light troops. In the first day's march
he reached Anchialus, a town said to have been founded by the

king of Assyria, Sardanapalus. The fortifications, in their mag-
nitude and extent, still in Arrian's time, bore the character of
greatness, which the Assyrians appear singularly to have affected
in works of the kind.   A monument representing Sardanapalus
was found there, warranted by an inscription in Assyrian cha-
racters, of course in the old Assyrian language, which the Greeks,
whether well or ill, interpreted thus: ' Sardanapalus, son of
Anacyndaraxes, in one day founded Anchialus and Tarsus.   Eat,
drink, play: all other human joys are not worth a fillip.'   Sup-
posing this version nearly exact (for Arrian says it was not quite
so), whether the purpose has not been to invite to civil order
a people disposed to turbulence, rather than to recommend im-
moderate luxury, may perhaps reasonably be questioned.   What,
indeed, could be the object of a king of Assyria in founding such
towns in a country so distant from his capital, and so divided from
it by an immense extent of sandy deserts and lofty mountains, and,
still more, how the inhabitants could be at once in circumstances
to abandon themselves to the intemperate joys which their prince
has been supposed to have recommended, is not obvious; but it may
deserve observation that, in that line of coast, the southern of
Lesser Asia, ruins of cities, evidently of an age after Alexander,
yet barely named in history, at this day astonish the adventurous
traveller by their magnificence and elegance.   Amid the desolation which, under a singularly barbarian government, has for
so many centuries been daily spreading in the finest countries of
the globe, whether more from soil and climate, or from oppor-
tunities for commerce, extraordinary means must have been found
for communities to flourish there, whence it may seem that the
measures of Sardanapalus were directed by juster views than have

been commonly ascribed to him; but that monarch having been the last of a dynasty, ended by a revolution, obloquy on his memory would follow of course from the policy of his successors and their partisans.

" The inconsistency of traditions concerning Sardanapalus is striking in Diodorus's account of him."—*Mitford's Greece*, vol. ix. pp. 311, 312, and 313.

THE END.

Lightning Source UK Ltd.
Milton Keynes UK
08 June 2010

155327UK00006B/6/A